Choice

on Fire

Choice
on
Fire

ZACH JENKINS

Choice on Fire © Zach Jenkins.
Paperback Edition.
Design and formatting by Silver Heart Publishing.
ISBN-13:978-1542311243.
ISBN-10:1542311241.

This book contains sexually explicit content which is suitable only
for mature readers.

Contents

CHAPTER 1

Maxwell

THE HISS OF THE BUS' brakes jolted Maxwell Cope awake. He'd lost track of how long it'd been since he'd landed in Chicago. After the flight from Afghanistan, complete with several layover stops along the way, though, the bus ride was a comparatively short last leg of his journey. A quick look out the window confirmed that he was definitely in the suburbs of somewhere in the Midwest, home of strip malls and cities that were all basic carbon copies of each other.

Brick Swan better be worth it.

The familiar tingle of the first meeting with a new man

tickled the nerves in his stomach, and made him adjust his growing dick. If Brick was half as stunning as his pictures, Maxwell knew he was in for a good vacation, and, after his last few months, he was ready for a couple of weeks away from duty and the Army.

So far they had only exchanged emails, but that had been enough to convince Maxwell that Brick had the perfect personality to be a fun vacation fuck buddy. The topless photo that Brick had sent in an email sealed the deal. He'd originally been planning to visit a middle-aged man in San Diego instead. The guy was rich and had an enormous house with an indoor pool and easy access to the beach. Those were the kinds of guys Maxwell usually hooked up with.

But when Brick appeared in his dreams three nights in a row and Maxwell woke with almost painful erections, he'd been happy when his San Diego hookup had needed to postpone because of a work project. Maxwell had quickly made arrangements for a summer fling with Brick just outside of Chicago.

As he looked out at the boring Midwest, though, it confirmed that beaches and a mansion would be a great change of pace after the blandness of Illinois.

The sex with the hot fireman better be worth it.

Shaking off the last of his sleep, Maxwell grabbed his backpack and exited the bus. After the driver helped him find his duffel bag in the storage compartment, the bus pulled away, leaving Maxwell alone in a strange town where he'd once again be seducing a virtual stranger.

Maxwell loved the Army, everything from the chain of command to the tent cities. He was also a firm believer that the country, and even the world, needed people like him to keep the terrorists at bay. But when he was on leave, he did his best to push all of that aside. He certainly never went into details about his day-to-day Army life with civilians.

No one wants to know how the sausage is made. Just look macho, smile handsomely, and fuck this Brick guy for two weeks until it's time to go back. And no matter what, don't fall for him.

That last part was important. He knew soldiers who had relationships back in the States, and they were miserable because of the distance every single day. Staying unattached was the only way to survive what he did for the country.

Since Brick hadn't arrived to pick him up yet, Maxwell pulled his camera from his backpack, and started snapping pictures. From the bus stop, he could see down the hill that led to the river, and the rise of the hill on the other side. The Fox River, according to his research. He definitely wanted to get down there to take some pictures while Brick was at work.

Behind him was a fire station. He snapped a couple of quick shots, wondering if that was where Brick worked, but figured he'd have plenty of time to get some good ones of whichever station he worked at.

It might take some work to talk Brick into showing him off

there, but Maxwell had no doubt he could convince him. Most of his similar trips over the eleven years he'd been in the Army had ended with some poor man or woman begging him for a more serious commitment, even marriage.

Not that Maxwell was falling for any of that. His one rule was that he visit a different city every year. What was the point of being in the Army if not to see the world?

He scanned the area one more time for Brick before going back to looking at his surroundings through the display on his camera. Photography had started as a way to kill time during deployments, but had merged into something much more important as time passed and his skill increased. It was one thing he was good at that didn't involve killing someone or making them fall hard for him before he disappeared from their lives.

"Army man," a female called out from nearby. "You need some help?"

Maxwell smiled at the woman in her early twenties. She had purple hair, a white tank top, rainbow-striped skirt and combat boots that made her appear much younger.

Maxwell smiled. He had gone through that phase. Never a skirt, but he'd worn similar shorts one summer during high school when he'd first come out as gay before realizing that he was bisexual. He'd moved on from that phase soon afterward. Then there'd been the suit phase, the punk phase, and the sweatpants phase. He always moved on quickly. He'd been wearing mostly jeans and a T-shirt for a while and wondered if it wasn't time for another change.

"No, I'm fine," Maxwell said. He showed her his camera. "Just waiting for a friend."

She looked around dramatically. "I don't see no friend, man. You sure you don't need a ride? I don't bite."

"Didn't your parents teach you to stay away from strangers?" Maxwell asked while wondering if she might be hitting on him.

"Yeah, but my dad would beat my ass if he knew a soldier needed a little help and I didn't make it happen. He was Army, too. Retired now. My boyfriend gets off work before too long, so you better make up your mind before I run out of time."

Glancing at his watch, he realized that Brick was already twenty minutes late. That had never happened to him on one of his vacations before. Maybe Brick had left early when the bus took a few minutes longer than planned, leaving Maxwell on his own to get a ride.

Maxwell hoped Brick wasn't that kind of guy. He'd seemed so nice in the emails that he couldn't believe it. Something must have come up.

"Sure. If you know how to get to Madison Street, I'd love a ride."

She nodded and shook her keys at him. "That's just a couple blocks from my place."

The passenger seat of the old, unwashed car was a mess of burger wrappers and paper cups.

"One sec," she said, pushing past Maxwell, and started tossing the garbage to the back seat.

Maxwell, recovering from his initial shock, said, "Whoa. Don't just move it from one spot to another. There's a garbage can right here." He nudged her aside, grabbed a small pile of the trash, and dumped it in the black garbage can just a few feet away on the sidewalk. "See? Like a human, not like some kind of monkey."

The girl rolled her eyes. "God, you sound just like my dad. Who knew the Army made everyone anal retentive?"

She pitched in easily enough, though. Maxwell decided that the girl was all right. After all, she was helping him out without even knowing anything about him. After the seat was clear, they piled into the car and headed toward the river.

"What's your name?" he asked, breaking the silence.

"Nicole. What's *your* name, rank, and serial number, soldier?"

He playfully returned her earlier eye roll. "Maxwell Cope."

Nicole snorted before she had a chance to cover her face. "That's a ridiculous name, Max."

"Maxwell. Max is my dad," he said automatically.

Rather than taunting him further, she nodded seriously.

"So, what are you in town for?" she asked.

Sex. Two weeks of constant man-on-man love.

"I'm meeting a friend. A pen pal. We've been writing each other for several months and I had some leave, so here I am."

"Oh. So, sex. Fun."

Maxwell, normally hard to fluster, blushed at the girl's knowing glance.

"Well, I brought my camera, too. I'm going to walk around town and take pictures while he's working."

With the car still moving, the girl removed her hands from the steering wheel to clap with glee. "Take me with you. I'll show you all the good stuff. There's an old wind—"

"Steering wheel, please." Maxwell had seen plenty of combat during his time in the Army, but Nicole speeding down the crowded street, clapping and not looking at the road was the scariest thing he'd witnessed in ages. "Your dad will kill you if you kill a soldier, right?"

She stuck out her tongue, but at least her hands returned to the wheel.

Maxwell quickly added, "But I'd love to tag along with you and find some good spots for photos."

Since she'd already mentioned her boyfriend, Maxwell figured they must be serious and she wouldn't try to hit on him. An interesting woman like her probably had an amazing man and wouldn't be looking for anything other than friendship.

She swerved into a driveway. Maxwell verified the address matched the one he'd provided, and reached for the door handle.

"Give me your phone," she demanded. "I'll give you my number."

He handed her the phone. She quickly entered her own and then called herself. "There. Now we have each other's. I'll text you sometime and see what you're up to."

Maxwell turned to thank Nicole for the ride after he got out of the car, but she was already backing out of the driveway. "Good luck getting laid!" she screamed as she sped down the street.

Shaking his head at the strange woman, Maxwell tossed his backpack over one shoulder and his duffel bag over the other. When he reached the front door, he knocked and waited to meet Brick. That first moment was always touch and go. If a vacation was going to turn magical, he always knew in that first instant.

No one answered. Maxwell, growing frustrated at being stood up, checked the doorknob. He'd entered many houses in Afghanistan, usually with his fellow soldiers following right behind him. Depending on the mission, sometimes he'd bash the door down, and sometimes he'd enter silently.

He decided he should go the stealthy route in case Brick had a gun and was easily startled. Besides, if Brick was going to blow him off, he deserved to get the shit scared out of him.

He heard someone on TV screaming in a room on the back of the small ranch house. Maxwell loved horror flicks. Following the sound, he hoped that Brick was the kind of guy who got horny after having a good scare. Now that Maxwell was in Brick's house, he was desperate to make sure their brief time together started with a bang.

CHAPTER 2

Brick

B
RICK SWAN WATCHED THE LUBED and glistening
cock slide into the ready and willing ass. He'd
never get tired of seeing the penetration. He just
wished he were the one doing it.

His nerves were shot from worrying about the guest he'd
invited to spend two weeks at his house. They'd exchanged
plenty of emails, but that wasn't anything like meeting him
face-to-face. Brick was pretty sure the guy was interested in
him. At least it felt like Maxwell had flirted with him. He'd
seemed happy to get the picture of Brick shirtless.

Brick wished he'd pushed a little harder to confirm that

he was really coming with plans of dating rather than beating around the bush with innuendo.

Brick didn't know what he'd do if Maxwell was just visiting as a friend.

He can't be that clueless, right? I wish someone would tell me that I'm just being a nervous fool.

Glancing at the clock, Brick saw he still had about an hour before he needed to leave to pick up Maxwell.

I wish he'd just let me pick him up at the airport. Shit. What if that's a bad sign?

He had too much time to wait patiently and too little to really start much of anything else.

Might as well empty the chamber. I don't want to bust my nut in two seconds if he is interested in sex.

Before hitting play again, he checked out his own body. It had been months since he'd trained for his last bodybuilding competition. The dieting had proven too much to endure. He just liked food too much. His body still looked great, though, he thought. He had never liked the creepy veins that had started showing right before he stopped competing.

Thick and solid is the way to go.

The stray thought reminded him to hit play. His own swollen cock twitched as the big muscly dude slid into the smaller man. The smaller man uttered the kind of groan that Brick was desperate to hear in real life. He clicked on his laptop to watch the moment of penetration several more times before setting the computer on the nearby coffee table so the men could get back to fucking while Brick resumed stroking himself.

Normally masturbating made Brick lonely. Today was different, though. The prospect of a new man in his life had him excited in ways beyond just his physical needs.

What if Maxwell ends up being the one?

Brick worked on his much-needed release so he could get cleaned up and head to the bus stop. He wanted to get there a few minutes early so he'd be able to see Maxwell the second he got off the bus.

Focusing on the scene rather than how perfect the next two weeks might be as long as he didn't screw things up, Brick grunted in time with his strokes, which were in time with the video. It was like he was fucking the smaller man and was pounding him so hard that the guy's dick was flopping between his legs because he couldn't even focus on stroking his own cock.

Brick's legs tightened. He only needed a few more seconds.

"Well, well, couldn't even wait for me to get here, huh? Brick Swan, I hope. I'm Maxwell Cope. I'd shake your hand, but that dick of yours is looking pretty welcoming too."

Eyes wide with terror and embarrassment, Brick covered as much as he could with his hands and prayed it was all just a horrible dream.

The man claiming to be Maxwell was several inches shorter than Brick, but was clearly in amazing shape. He reminded

Brick of some of the MMA fighters he trained with once in a while. Wiry, quick as hell, and could have you tapping for submission before you really noticed they'd started moving. This guy had the body and the swagger. Despite Brick's own strength, he'd bet money that he wouldn't last one round against him in a fight.

But I sure'd like to spend a few minutes wrestling with him.

Brick had only seen a couple of pictures of Maxwell, but the buzzed hair, dark tan, and strong jawline were definitely recognizable. His eyes looked more intense in person. As if they were looking through Brick, around corners, and even behind his own body without needing to move.

Brick forced himself to move his hands from his dick to behind his head and at least pretend to be relaxed. He'd hoped that Maxwell would be interested in fooling around, and he certainly wasn't running away.

"Holy shit," Brick said. "Great to see you. What are you...I thought you still had another hour."

"Nope. Must have been a time zone mix-up." He didn't even look mad at the mistake, fortunately. Instead he looked horny and ready to play. "But what a pleasant one. Let me give you a hand."

Maxwell dropped his bags on the floor and climbed right onto Brick's legs. He looked great in his t-shirt and jeans, but Brick felt severely underdressed as Maxwell's clothed body pinned his naked legs to the couch.

Before Brick could ask him to undress, too, Maxwell wrapped his hands around Brick's dick and slowly started stroking, stealing Brick's breath away.

Brick's mouth hung open in shock at his daring guest. Maxwell had both of his strong hands wrapped around Brick's shaft at the same time and was twisting them in opposite directions while they moved up and down. In just a matter of seconds, Maxwell had already become Brick's favorite boyfriend ever.

Whoa. Getting ahead of yourself, aren't you?

"You going to come for me, big guy? Come on. Get your jizz all over my hands."

Brick decided that he needed to find a way to make two weeks last forever, but any actual plans to make that happen would have to come later. The filthy talk was pushing him quickly to the edge of his orgasm.

"That dick's going to look great when it fills up my ass later tonight."

Maxwell continued talking, making Brick gasp and blush in shock even as his dick continued to get harder. He closed his eyes because his body was freaking out from sensory overload. Maxwell did something with his thumb on the tip of his dick that created sensations that shot through his body that just weren't possible while his other hand continued pumping him with its tight grip.

Brick opened his eyes to try and figure out what Maxwell was doing.

Their eyes locked.

Brick had time to notice that they were brown, but when Maxwell smiled and ordered, "Come for me," Brick had no option but to comply.

He heard the profanities flowing from his own mouth but couldn't understand the words he was saying. Cum exploded from his dick, shooting in a high arc before gravity pulled it down against his waxed chest. His body shook, but Maxwell managed to stay straddled on top of his legs, refusing to be cast aside.

"Damn," Brick finally managed to say when he regained control of his mouth. "Welcome to my house. How was the trip?"

"It just got a whole lot better, Brick. It was already well worth the miserable flight."

The awkwardness of being naked around a man who was fully dressed flooded back. "I've gotta be honest. I'm not sure what we do next, but I should probably clean up."

"Solid plan," Maxwell said, but didn't move.

"Umm...could you..."

Maxwell shook his head. "It seems like a big, strong man like you wouldn't need my permission to get up from his own couch and put his clothes on."

The words sounded playful, but there seemed to be a rough edge beneath them.

I'm just imagining things. The guy's been traveling forever. He's probably exhausted.

Brick chose to believe that Maxwell just wanted to feel Brick's strength. Men and women all seemed to enjoy watching him just be strong. Hell, that attention was half the reason he worked out as often as he did. With a dramatic grunt, Brick swung his legs off the couch, and easily rose to his feet, carrying Maxwell with him.

"Thanks for actually showing up," Brick said. "I've been worrying that you wouldn't show up for a while now. It's great to see you. You look even better in person."

"Thanks. You, too. But you never did send me any pictures of you naked. That's some nice equipment, Brick. Goddamn, we're going to have some fun for the next two weeks."

"Hell," Brick said. "If things go well, two weeks can be just the beginning, right?"

Maxwell dropped to the ground. "Yeah, man. Sure." His body language quickly changed from open and excited to closed and shy.

Shit. That was too much, too fast. Chill out.

Maxwell sat back down on the couch. "Why don't you get cleaned up? I'm going to rest here for a little bit. It was a long trip. I'll grab a couple beers for us if you have some in the fridge. If not, you can take me out to get some when you are more presentable for going out in public."

Brick suddenly felt very naked in front of Maxwell. He needed to shower and put on clean clothes afterward. He still grabbed his dirty clothes from where he'd tossed them around the room. There was no sense in being lazy and leaving things where they didn't belong.

Just before leaving the room, he turned back to Maxwell. After Maxwell's reaction to the joke of them staying together for longer than the brief vacation, he didn't even want to ask. In the end, his desire to have his friends meet his new hot boyfriend, if even only for just two weeks, won over. "Hey, I forgot to send you an email. Some friends are having a get-together later tonight. I told them you'd be too tired, but they made me promise to invite you. What do you say?"

He didn't answer right away. Brick was just about to tell him not to worry about it when Maxwell finally spoke. "I slept most of the flight, and after that," he said, patting the couch cushion, "I won't be falling asleep for a while. So, why not? Let's go meet the friends. I'll see if I can't get you riled up for a second round by the time we're ready to leave the party and come home."

Brick's heart pounded with excitement. He'd finally have a date worth bringing to visit with his friends and not feel like the fifth wheel.

Maxwell quickly added. "Just give me a few minutes to catch my breath. How long until we leave?"

Brick glanced at the clock. "A little over an hour."

Maxwell rose and started heading toward the door. Brick wondered if he'd just realized he'd left a bag outside.

"Okay. Let me go outside and take some pictures. That'll help me settle down and get back into proper vacation mode before you show me off to your friends. A little fresh air will do me good. I'll be back in thirty minutes. Then I'll clean up and off we'll go. Deal?"

Brick couldn't say no. And as much as he wanted Maxwell to join him in the shower, he tried to convince himself that it might be for the best to slow down and get to know each other a little more before fooling around again. "Yeah, man. Sounds like a plan. I'll see you in a few. Hey, before you go, tell me something real about yourself. That's what we need, right? To balance out all the sex? Where are you from?"

"Idaho," Maxwell answered briskly, looking like he needed to get outside as soon as possible.

Brick wondered if he needed a smoke and didn't want Brick to know about it. Or maybe he was having some kind of bad military flashback.

Yes, taking time to get to know each other will be for the best.

"Idaho," Brick echoed. "I've always wanted to go up there and see the buffalo and wide open exanses."

"Yeah, it's something," Maxwell said quickly. "Okay. Back in a few."

Maxwell left Brick alone in his hall, naked, and hoping that the next two weeks weren't going to be such a crazy rollercoaster...and that Maxwell would actually come back from wherever he was going.

CHAPTER 3

Maxwell

AXWELL SPRINTED OUT THE DOOR so quickly that he didn't even notice that he'd forgotten his camera until he was halfway down the block. Cursing his mistake, he decided not to return for it. The lie about what state he was from still had him nearly shaking. Such an innocuous question and he'd still defaulted to lies. He was pretty sure he'd already told Brick that he was from Nebraska once in an email and little lies like that would get him in trouble when Brick caught him.

What difference does it make? It's just two weeks and I always lie. I'll just say I was born in one and raised in the other.

He couldn't place why it felt different this time. He tried chalking it up to jet lag, but knew that was just a convenient lie, and he hated lying to himself. There was some connection with Brick already and no amount of telling himself he was being stupid about what he was feeling was going to change that. *I need to keep a little distance and protect myself from falling for him.*

Stretching in the warm sun, Maxwell tried to shake it off. When in enemy territory, the first step was to relax. Tightening up led to mistakes and he didn't want to make any more with Brick. He'd seemed so nice in the emails, and meeting him in person hadn't diminished that impression one bit.

No matter what happened Maxwell needed to protect himself without hurting Brick.

Brick's house was only a block away from the river. Maxwell quickly covered the distance and started skipping stones and reminding himself what about Brick had attracted him to the man in the first place.

He always flirted in the emails, but never pushed for sex chats. Brick's flirting was always fun and made Maxwell feel better about himself. Unlike most of the men and women he'd dated in the past, Brick told Maxwell things about himself that weren't about how rich or powerful he was. He was more likely to joke about the ingrown hair from getting his chest waxed than brag about saving people from a fire.

It all made Maxwell feel like Brick wanted *him* instead

21

of just wanting to fuck him for a couple of weeks. He sternly reminded himself to loosen up and have fun while he was at Brick's instead of running away all the time, and hoped he'd be able to follow through with that.

"What's up, Sergeant?" Nicole shouted from a nearby park bench.

Maxwell instantly regretted letting her drive him to Brick's. As much as he wanted something different from Brick than he'd had from his other lovers, he knew the odds of it turning into something permanent were nonexistent. Maxwell just wasn't relationship material. He probably couldn't blame his dad for that anymore, but it certainly didn't help. Nicole was another person he was already starting to like a little too much, and she'd just be another connection in a town he'd probably never return to.

Still, he couldn't help but smile as she bounced over to join him. "I thought you had a hot date with your boyfriend?"

"Likewise," she replied, picking up a rock and tossing it in a high arc into the river. "Mine is working a little late to cover for someone who went home sick. He needs the overtime for beer money. Where's yours?"

"In the shower."

Nicole threw back her head to laugh and gently shoved Maxwell. "Damn, you work fast."

"Not going to talk about it," he said, tossing another rock into the river.

"Fine, you fuddy duddy, but I'm twenty-three. I might look young, but I can handle whatever you can dish out."

They stood in silence while Maxwell skipped a few stones. He knew that if he just kind of wandered away, it would probably end any future conversations with Nicole. Still, he found himself asking, "Why do you have all this free time during the day? Shouldn't you be working in an office somewhere?"

The girl shrugged, suddenly looking sad. "No. I work dinner shifts. I wasn't very good in school, so I didn't waste the money on college, which is biting me in the ass now when I apply for jobs."

"You could join the military," Maxwell suggested.

Nicole snorted. "The military complex? Fuck that. I mean, it was great for my dad, and you, I guess. But I'm not cut out for following the Man's rules, you know?"

"Jesus Christ. What are they teaching you people around here? Listen, I had shitty grades in school, and no prospects for my future. I signed up for the Army and it helped me get my act together. Now I have a great, guaranteed job until I retire, and after that I'll have the GI Bill to take some classes and start up a second career."

"You ever consider becoming a recruiter with all that rhetoric? What are you going to study?" Nicole tossed a rock into the river, underhand and with a high arc. The stone made a plop sound and disappeared. "Shit. How do you do that?"

"You have to throw it sidearm." Maxwell showed her the

motion and then threw a rock that skipped three times before sinking. "I'm not sure what I'll be studying."

"Some plan you've got."

"I'll be retired young. Probably around forty. The government will be cutting me checks for the rest of my life. I'll study whatever the fuck strikes my fancy." Maxwell had no idea why he was pushing so hard. It wasn't like he knew Nicole enough to care what she did with her life.

"Hmm. Very interesting."

Happy that she was intrigued but hadn't asked any questions, Maxwell left her alone to her thoughts. He had no plans to badger her into signing up. He certainly wasn't a recruiting officer.

When she chucked another rock into the river, he stepped up behind her.

With one hand on her hip, he grabbed her right hand and guided her through the proper throwing motion. "The key is to come in flat and then flick your wrist like this."

Her hair smelled like strawberry shampoo. With her edgy attitude, she was the kind of woman he was frequently attracted to. He loved loner rebels like himself. But other than a mild interest in helping a fellow lost soul, he had no plans of making a move on her. That was against his vacation rules. The man or woman he was with for those two weeks was the only person in the world that mattered.

Plus, except for the stupid little moment of panic earlier,

he really was looking forward to spending time with Brick as long as he could talk himself out of running away every few minutes.

Nicole's next rock skipped once. She squealed with delight, but her next two sank immediately. Maxwell touched her arm, preparing to show her the motion again.

"Get your hands of my woman, dick!" a gruff voice shouted behind them.

"Billy, no. It's not like that," Nicole said, turning to face the man.

"Like hell it isn't." Billy stormed toward them with his fists balled.

Stepping in front of Nicole, Maxwell stood with his feet shoulder-width apart and his arms calmly at his side. Billy was tall, but about twenty pounds overweight. He looked like the kind of guy who had grown up bullying smaller kids and saw Maxwell as an easy target.

Maxwell used to have trouble with a guy like Billy. That was before the Army taught him how to fight.

"Calm down, Billy," Maxwell said, standing his ground while trying to not look threatening. "I was just showing her how to skip rocks." When Billy didn't slow, Maxwell added, "I'm gay, dude." It wasn't the complete truth since he liked women, too, but Billy didn't need to know that at the moment. "It's not like you have anything to worry about."

Billy made a face as if he'd just bitten into an onion. "Come on, Nicki. Let's get out of here. You don't want to be hanging out with sissies like him."

Maxwell planned three different ways he could break Billy's arm while getting him to the ground, but forced himself to hold his place. He didn't want to cause any trouble for Nicole by confronting the guy. Unless the boyfriend did something that would actually hurt Nicole, it wasn't any of his business. Billy would be around long after Maxwell had moved on, and he certainly looked like the type who would hold a grudge.

"Knock it off, Billy," Nicole said weakly. "Maxwell just got into town and doesn't know many people here. He's Army like my dad so we started talking. That's all."

"Shit," Billy said, spitting to the side. "I forgot they let the gays in. Stupid liberals, watering down our military."

Maxwell wanted to shove the words down Billy's throat, but he'd learned to endure much worse taunting from much more formidable men.

"Sorry, Maxwell," Nicole said. "I gotta go. Billy and I have plans tonight."

"Kegger!" Billy screamed, the thought of beer already making him forget about the threat to his woman.

Wondering what Nicole was doing with an asshole like Billy, Maxwell nodded at her. "I'll catch you around town, I'm sure. I'll be out taking photos whenever I get the chance."

"Oh, there's a windmill about a mile downriver. We should go check it out tomorrow."

Before Maxwell could agree, Billy tugged his girlfriend's arm. Dragging her toward his truck, he said, "Let's go. They'll be tapping the keg any minute now."

Nicole was dating a jerk, but didn't appear to be in any imminent danger, so Maxwell let her go, hoping that Billy wasn't as big a jerk as he appeared at first glance. While skipping a few more stones, he listened, waiting for her to cry out for help, almost wishing for it so he could put Billy in his place. When he heard the truck pull away with no further incident, he shook his head and decided to walk back to Brick's and avoid any chance of getting involved in any other problems.

Meeting Brick's friends was going to be scary enough. He should have declined. Maxwell normally looked to date loners like himself. People who preferred watching TV at home or quiet dinners in the corner booth of dark restaurants. He knew it was silly since it was easy enough to disappear after his vacation was up, but it still made it easier to break away afterward if he didn't make any friends.

"He's a fireman," Maxwell said out loud. "I should have known better. Those guys are probably as tight as we are in the Army."

Thinking about just how different this trip was going to be compared to his previous ones, Maxwell thought about his strategy while returning to the house.

As he pushed through the door and heard Brick singing a Metallica song, he decided that he'd try and embrace whatever

Brick wanted to throw at him. He'd smile and pretend to be the perfect boyfriend around Brick's friends, rather than trying to keep Brick away from them when they were together. It was hard to imagine Brick's friends not being amazing like he was.

One more thing that will hurt when I leave, but whatever. I'm not afraid of a little pain.

Besides, Brick was so adorable, trying to growl along with the lead singer, that Maxwell wanted to do whatever would make him happy.

This is going to be a very different kind of fling.

Forcing himself not to try to seduce Brick into bed and away from his friends, he cheerily said, "Five minutes. I'll be showered and dressed. You can time it. If I'm wrong, I'll do whatever you want when we get back."

Brick stopped singing and asked, "And what if you *do* finish in less than five?"

"Well, I'll do whatever you want, anyway." Maxwell said, happy to be back to flirting.

"Sounds like my kind of bet," Brick said as he hurried to the kitchen and set the timer on the microwave. "Go!"

Maxwell sprinted to the bathroom. He was done and dressed in four minutes.

"They teach you that in the Army? Do a bunch of you guys get naked and practice that fast shower together?" Brick asked, still pulling his socks on.

Maxwell ignored the question. "Hurry up, slowpoke. I want to meet these friends of yours and see if they're real people or not."

The last of Maxwell's immediate worries washed away in the shower. He wasn't going to let Billy, or his own fears of falling too hard for Brick, upset him and ruin his trip. Maxwell was on vacation and was determined have a good time.

CHAPTER 4

Brick

"Wow. This house belongs on one of those sitcoms with the perfect happy families," Maxwell said as they pulled into the driveway at Clay and Ezra's house.

Brick looked at the green house with the big porch with fresh eyes. With the old trees and perfectly manicured lawn decorated with perfectly arranged flowers, it certainly had a lot of charm, even if it wasn't really his style.

"They got the house for free, too. Ezra's mom gave it to them a little while back. Lucky bastards."

"Jesus. Think she'd adopt me?"

The thought of anyone being in charge of Maxwell made Brick laugh. "Probably. Alice is a sweetheart. She practically adopts everyone she meets. But she doesn't have any more houses to give away. Before we go in: Clay and Ezra own the place. Clay is a firefighter. Ezra is a beautician. David and Quinn are dating and practically married, it seems. David's a fireman. Quinn is a teacher. They have a son. Brian. From Quinn's first marriage. David and Clay work together but in a different city than me. What else..." Brick wracked his brain for other important information.

"Relax, man." Maxwell patted Brick's arm reassuringly. "I've been in real, honest-to-God, close quarters combat. This will be a piece of cake." Maxwell opened the door a couple of inches before turning back and saying, "Oh, dude. Do you think they'll have cake? I haven't had any in like a year."

Maxwell's confident words helped Brick relax a little. He knew he was being silly, but the two couples waiting inside seemed to have the perfect relationships, and Brick was desperate to have one of his own someday. He wasn't quite ready to pick out curtains with Maxwell, but he wanted to finally be able to introduce someone to his friends who would make them take notice...in a good way, for once.

And he did freak out a little bit already back at my place. I hope this isn't a horrible idea.

"Yeah, you're right," he said, more to convince himself. "It's just a get-together. You like brats and burgers?"

Maxwell's eyes went wide. "I can't eat that. I'm a vegetarian."

"Shit. I should have asked. I think Ezra will—"

"Just kidding, Brick. We eat whatever they slop onto our trays over in Afghanistan. This is going to be a fucking paradise to eat some good meat here before I take you home and make you give me some more good meat for dessert."

Maxwell was out of the car before Brick started to blush, but his cheeks were still warm when they walked around back to join his friends on the deck.

All four men screamed his name when they saw him. Introductions were an overwhelming whirlwind of questions and stories designed to poke fun at Brick. Fortunately, Maxwell seemed to notice that he was flustered. He sent Brick off to find beer in the fridge while he fielded questions.

When Brick returned, Maxwell was helping Clay at the grill. The two men were laughing about something. Trying not to be the kind of guy who had to constantly hang around his date, Brick sat down with the other guys.

"Soooooooooo," Ezra began, stretching the word out longer than necessary. "He's finally here. Anything serious? He's the Army guy, right? Does he—"

"Down, boy," David said to Ezra. "Take a breath and let him answer a couple questions before firing off more of them."

"Sorry." Ezra flashed a sheepish smile. "It's been so long

since someone brought a new man around. But fine. First question. Are you two serious?"

Brick took a drink before answering. "Not yet. We just met." Before Ezra had a chance to ask another round of questions, Brick waved him down. He couldn't remember which of his friends knew what about Maxwell, so he started at the beginning. "I probably told you all this already, but he's in the Army. He's been deployed for a while. We met through one of those pen pal programs. He happened to have a couple weeks of vacation, so he flew in this afternoon and here we are."

Quinn interrupted. "Wait. He flew in and the first thing you did was bring him over to meet us?"

Brick blushed again and shot a glance over at Maxwell who was stretching, which exposed the hard muscles of his stomach. "Not exactly..."

The whole table started laughing and sneaking glances at Maxwell, too.

Quinn eventually calmed himself long enough to say, "So we're just a little downtime before you guys get back to the real action. That sounds exciting."

Brick knew another round of questions was coming and they'd get more personal the longer he continued answering them. Afraid that he'd be silently judged when he didn't have the answers to things like what kind of music Maxwell liked, Brick called over to his date. "Here's your beer."

"Thanks, hon. I'll grab it in a sec."

"Guys, you're not going to believe this," Clay said. "This crazy bastard is like the lead man when they have to storm into terrorist houses and take out the bad guys."

"You kidding me?" David asked.

Maxwell shook his head. "But it's not as big of a deal as it sounds. We're armored up to the max and there are so many of us that usually go in. We hit them so hard and so fast, they normally just surrender. Besides, it's not like we're doing it every day. Most days, we're just hanging out on base, trying to keep ourselves busy so we don't go crazy from boredom."

Ezra cocked his head. "Sounds a little like firemen, but with less farting."

Maxwell laughed. "Don't count on it."

"Are you getting out soon? Maybe moving in with Brick?" David asked.

Brick's friend was just trying to help, but the question grated Brick's nerves. First of all, Brick didn't know how much longer Maxwell would be in the Army. Second, Brick worried that any small chance of the two of them having a future might fall apart if he or his friends applied too much pressure. It was way too early in their relationship for questions like that.

Hell, it was too early to even call it a relationship.

"The food almost ready?" Brick asked Clay.

"Fine, fine, we get it," Clay said. "Too personal. How about this one? Max, do you want cheese on your burger?"

"Sure," Maxwell said, sitting down next to Brick and giving his thigh a gentle squeeze. "Please call me Maxwell, though. My dad's the only Max I know."

"Oh, sorry," Clay said while adding cheese to the hamburgers. "You don't get along with your dad?"

Maxwell shrugged off the question.

Brick watched, fascinated. Without saying a word, he was learning more about Maxwell than when the two of them actually talked. His own parents had moved to Florida years ago, but he'd always gotten along with them well enough. But he knew guys like David who weren't that lucky.

What did his dad do to him?

"That's too bad," Clay said as he scooped the meat onto a serving tray.

"You think so?" Maxell snapped more abruptly than the situation called for in Brick's opinion. "You don't even know the guy. What if he's in prison for murdering a bunch of teachers or something?"

The silence that followed was stifling. Brick wanted to tell Clay to stop, but he also wanted to see what the line of questions might reveal. When Clay, probably just trying to break the tension, asked, "Did he?" Brick nodded in support of the question.

"Of course not." Maxwell was practically gritting his teeth. "But that doesn't mean he's a good guy. There's a lot of shades of gray between saint and serial killer."

Clay's mouth hung open in shock at the cold tone in Maxwell's voice.

David spoke up. "I hear you, Maxwell. My dad constantly reminded me that I was an idiot most of my childhood."

Brick let out a breath he'd been holding, sure that the conversation would turn to David long enough for Maxwell to calm down.

Instead, Maxwell asked, "Were you?"

Ezra and Quinn both gasped.

Brick felt a bead of sweat roll down the side of his face. He didn't wipe it away for fear of attracting any attention, hoping that the moment would just pass without any further ado.

What the hell is he thinking talking to my friends like that? Is he trying to make them hate him?

Despite his impulse to drag him away to yell at him, Brick could only watch the man who was supposed to be his boyfriend, but was really little more than a stranger, acting like an ass in front of people Brick cared about.

Fortunately, Quinn, ever the teacher, jumped in to save the day. "Maxwell, dear, please remember that everyone's personal tragedies are important to them. You don't know anything about David's past and he doesn't know anything about yours. But if we're just going to lash out and belittle each other's experiences, we will never learn anything, will we? Now, can you pass me that ketchup and tell us about where you are stationed? I think you said Afghanistan?"

Maxwell turned his glare on Quinn. The two were nearly the same size, but all similarities ended there. Quinn taught grade school for a living. Maxwell looked mad enough to eat the kids in his class.

Brick couldn't believe the simple lunch had turned into an angry staredown, with Maxwell looking like a wild animal ready to attack Quinn. Not that David would allow that to happen, of course. Quinn's giant fiancé had already puffed out his chest. Clay, nearly as big as David, turned his full attention to the table, watching for any sudden movements.

Maxwell certainly didn't seem intimidated. Brick still didn't know exactly what Maxwell did in the Army. Most of what he knew, he'd just learned moments before. Maxwell had always found ways to dodge that topic in their emails. But whatever it was, Brick wasn't surprised it involved being able to clear out rooms of people just by himself.

Everyone flinched when Maxwell raised his hands into the air until they realized he was surrendering.

"Shit, guys, I'm so fucking sorry. I have no excuse. I always seem to get a little edgy when I first get back in the States for some reason, but that was just shitty beyond belief. Let's just say I have daddy issues and move on, okay? Forgive me, please. I'll be fine tomorrow, I'm sure. The thing with my name...just call me Maxwell or Cope, even. Just not Max, please."

"Sure," Quinn said quickly, with his hand on David's arm to prevent him from taking a step forward. "Maxwell Cope sounds like a name made for the military. I'm sure it suits you well." He set a bun on his plate, and in a perfectly normal voice asked, "So, Afghanistan?"

Maxwell ate half his burger in one bite and slowly chewed while everyone waited. "Yeah. I've been deployed out there a few times now. We do a fair amount of patrolling the streets and looking for scumbag terrorists. We're like a pack of wolves hunting for monsters. Sometimes I forget how to be civilized."

When he shoved the rest of the burger into his mouth, Brick filled the silence and tried to humanize his visitor. He didn't want his friends to think he'd gone entirely crazy inviting the wild soldier into his house. "Maxwell's into photography, too. He has a pretty fancy camera. I'm sure it takes better photos than my phone."

"What kind of photos do you do?" Ezra asked, perking up. "If you are looking for some subjects, you could come do some before and after pictures of the ladies that come to my salon. They'd adore it."

Maxwell swallowed. "Normally hollowed-out buildings, recently. There's a million of them over there. Fuck, I'm doing it again." Maxwell leaned forward in his chair and bounced his knee anxiously. "I don't really do photos of a lot of people. Hell, I barely hang around people most of the time. Big surprise there, right? I'm more into landmarks. Buildings mostly. But parks and rivers and things like that, too. I seem to gravitate to quiet places that have seen the chaos of war. But, I'd love to come over sometime when Brick's working over the next few days. I'll promise to behave."

Ezra laughed. "Dude, with that body and those tattoos, the ladies at the salon will forgive you for being a little rough around the edges. But I really do hope you are able to relax while you're here. You seem like you're still hyper-alert and ready for combat. Focus on the R&R. Make Brick show you a good time."

"Sir, yes, sir!" Maxwell barked while flashing a salute. "You're absolutely right. Brick was already doing a great job of helping me unwind before we came over here."

All four of his friends turned their attention to Brick with their eyebrows raised. He was happy that things were cooling down with Maxwell, but now he was going to have to field a million questions as soon as they got him alone.

When Maxwell had first shown up at his house, Brick had warmed quickly to Maxwell's impulsiveness. But out on the town, the erratic behavior wasn't proving to be nearly as fun.

Stifling a yawn, Maxwell asked, "Hey, can you take me home? Sorry to bail so soon, guys, but it *has* been a really long day."

Brick stood, perhaps a bit too quickly. "Sure, man. Let's get you some sleep." He waved his hand at his still-full plate, "Thanks for the food, guys. Sorry to not-really-eat and run..." He cut off as he heard himself rambling. "Well. Good night."

Brick followed after Maxwell, who was already marching

to the car. He'd text everyone later to apologize for the abrupt departure, but at the moment, he just needed to get away and try to catch his breath.

CHAPTER 5

Maxwell

MAXWELL WAS USED TO HAVING occasional outbursts back at camp. All the soldiers had them from time to time. But he'd always been able to suppress them during vacation. Vacations were all about the show, the sex, and getting out of town without falling for anyone.

The twenty-minute ride back to Brick's house felt like it took twenty hours. On the way in, they'd chatted and joked freely. The return trip passed in silence, leaving Maxwell worried that he'd ruined his trip on the first day, all because he couldn't shut his goddamn mouth and eat his cheeseburger.

I should have just fucked him in the shower, gone to bed, and let him visit his friends alone.

Based on Brick's white knuckles from his tight grip on the steering wheel, Maxwell knew he wasn't out of the woods yet, and he didn't know Brick well enough to figure out the best way to proceed.

He leaned his head against the window, pretending to be more tired than he was, and taking time to ponder why he seemed so set on sabotaging his time with a man who seemed perfect.

He lamely told himself that he didn't want to hurt Brick by dying on him some day, but knew it was really his own heart he was trying to protect. Why would Brick want to stay with him when he could only be around on vacations? What kind of relationship could that be?

When Brick pulled into the driveway, he parked outside the garage, pressed the garage door opener and said, "I'm going to go lift some weights for a little bit. You can go inside and do whatever. If you want to get some sleep, the bed in the spare room is already made up. Make yourself at home."

He's the kind of guy that needs some time alone to gather himself. I can respect that.

Maxwell nodded, deciding that lying low was in his best interest. He passed through the garage ahead of Brick, and entered the house alone.

Taking a few minutes to really examine the house for the

first time, he learned that it was a cute enough ranch-style home, but nothing to write home about. The place itself certainly wouldn't make it worth the trip, unlike the mansions that he frequently stayed at during his rendezvous.

What the house lacked in money, though, it more than made up for with the sexy fireman. If Maxwell could just quit screwing things up, the trip promised to be the best one ever.

He tried turning on the TV, but gave up when he couldn't figure out the magic combination of button presses that would get something to show on the screen. The world sure had changed in some bizarre ways since he'd joined the Army. He noticed it each time he came back to the States for any amount of time. With each trip back, it took a little longer to learn all the new nuances of the modern world. By the time he retired, he wouldn't be able to do anything. No one would want to hire him for anything.

The sad thoughts reminded Maxwell of how lonely he was most of the year. He needed these little vacations to make himself feel wanted.

And right now, my only hope of affection is out lifting weights instead of in here paying attention to me.

Grabbing his camera, he headed back out to the garage. Brick, curling a dumbbell loaded with weights, didn't even look up to acknowledge him. Just being in the same room together was already making Maxwell feel a little better, though.

He pointed his camera at the shelves around the garage

and started quickly snapping pictures without worrying much about quality. Just the process was therapeutic, and sometimes he took some of the most amazing photos when he didn't overthink it.

When Maxwell took pictures of a box of nails, Brick said, "You'll have to let me have copies of those for insurance purposes if I ever get robbed. What are you doing, man? You aren't even giving the camera time to focus."

"The camera doesn't need time to focus," Maxwell said while continuing to snap away. "The camera doesn't judge good or bad, it just observes."

"What kind of Buddhist camera are you using?"

Maxwell hadn't even really realized what he'd said so Brick's comment caught him off guard, making him laugh. "The Dalai Camera, of course."

Brick groaned. "I hope your photos are better than your jokes."

We're talking again.

Hoping to move past the disastrous meal, Maxwell tried to return to flirting. It had seemed to work so well when they'd first met. "My photos are top notch when I have something worth shooting. But these shelves are not really moving me. I need something inspiring."

Maxwell pretended that he was thinking about what in the garage might inspire him before he turned the camera toward Brick and snapped a few pictures. "Oh, this might work.

Maybe. A little diamond in the rough, but if I get the light just right...No, this won't do at all."

Brick's brow furrowed. "Why not? What's wrong with me?"

He sounded irritated, but Maxwell was pretty sure that he'd led him down the perfect path.

"Because you're a man of power and action, Brick. Not some dull stationary object like those nails. Your beauty lies in movement and strength. Why don't you do some more of those curls and we'll see how that looks?"

Brick grinned as he picked up the dumbbell.

There we go.

Maxwell walked in a large circle around the weight bench, stopping to take a more deliberate picture each time. He eventually forgot to use the camera's display as Brick's steady, effortless motion lifted and lowered the weight like some kind of industrial machine. His bicep swelling and then extending in time with Maxwell's pounding heart.

Brick, watching him the entire time, smiled as he noticed the effect he was having on Maxwell.

Maxwell cleared his throat. "No. This isn't right either. I mean, it's better, but it's not quite right. Why don't you take off your shirt?"

"Okay, but only if you do, too."

Maxwell was going to protest. He was enjoying being in charge of what he hoped was their foreplay. But he changed his mind when he realized that he was perfectly happy to do what Brick asked. It felt strange because Maxwell normally took the lead and showed his partners a passion they had never experienced, but Brick seemed perfectly suited for showing Maxwell a thing or two, too.

Feeling slightly vulnerable, and completely excited, he removed his shirt, set it on a shelf, and said, "Your turn."

Brick slowly undid each button on his shirt while Maxwell took pictures, frustrated that the lighting wasn't quite right, and moving around to try and find a better spot to get the shot he wanted.

"You doing okay there, Ansel Adams?"

"Is that the only photographer you know of?"

Brick finished removing his shirt. A light sheen of sweat covered his waxed chest. The smooth chest had surprised Maxwell when Brick had sent the shirtless photo a while back. Brick didn't seem like the sort of guy that would be into manscaping.

Not that I'm complaining. The guy looks like he should be posing on stage and flexing those beastly muscles.

Still, as perfect as Brick looked, it wasn't showing up on the pictures because of the damn lighting. He pressed the buttons to open the garage door to let in a little outside light.

Brick reached for his shirt, but before he could start putting it back on and cover that incredible body, Maxwell explained, "I need more light."

"The neighbors—"

"They aren't even going to notice, and if they do, well, they'll be happy for the show. Now lie down and show me what you can bench press."

"Okay, but make it quick."

"We already did a quick one, we should try a little slower this time."

Instead of complaining, Brick lay down and grabbed the bar.

"How much is that?" Maxwell asked, moving to where he'd stand if he were a spotter.

"Two-forty-five." Brick rubbed his hands against the bar while settling his grip.

Maxwell had only lifted that amount a few times in his life, and never more than twice at a time. He normally focused on weight that he could handle through more reps to focus on his endurance. Their patrols usually lasted for hours, and it wouldn't do at all to not have the strength he needed at the end of the night.

"You sure you don't need a spotter?"

"No. Not for this."

Brick breathed in. His chest puffed up as he braced for the weight. With a light grunt, he easily lifted the bar off the support and lowered it smoothly, completely in control, to his chest, and then exploded in a powerful thrust that pushed the barbell into the air. He lowered it slowly again, but before pushing it back up, he asked, "Aren't you supposed to be taking pictures?"

The raw power had caught Maxwell off guard.

"Right. I think this lighting will be fine."

Brick smiled, looking proud to have distracted Maxwell for a second.

As Brick completed a few more reps, Maxwell realized that the barbell kept getting in the way of the shot, disrupting the camera's focus. He moved to the side of the bench to take a couple of shots. Brick's laid-out body was a sight to behold, but it was missing the intensity in his eyes.

"Hold on a second. I want to get a shot. Don't drop anything."

Without asking for permission, Maxwell straddled Brick and sat down low on his stomach. "Hey, I'm sorry about earlier. I really will be fine." Maxwell paused. There were so many stray thoughts flying around in his head, from his dad, to how nice Brick's friends were, to how amazing he thought Brick was. But how could he explain the claustrophobia all of them caused him to feel without it being insulting to Brick.

Fortunately, Brick nodded and said, "Don't worry. I've already forgotten about it. I'm just glad you're here."

Aiming the camera at Brick's face, he said, "Okay, lift it again."

Brick went through a few more reps. Maxwell zoomed in

on his face. "Jesus, man, you look perfect right now. Like, a god or something. I've never seen anyone look this amazing. You should be a model. I can't wait to get them on my computer and see what I can do with the light."

Brick smiled and said, "If you can do half as well with the light as you can with turning me on, I can't wait to see them, either."

Maxwell shifted back to change the angle and felt Brick's dick press against his ass.

"Well, well. Do you always get hard-ons when you lift weights?"

"Only when evil devils are sliding on top of me and talking about how great I look."

Maxwell beamed at the reaction he'd caused and was thrilled at how abruptly the mood had recovered between them.

"You know what I really need is a picture of you naked and hard. *That* would be something amazing."

Maxwell had meant the words as just more flirty banter, figuring that he'd never agree. He almost fell off the bench when Brick nodded.

"Inside," Brick growled. "We'll do it in my bedroom."

Maxwell barely managed to stop himself from asking if Brick was serious. If the big, sexy host wanted to get naked and let him take pictures, Maxwell certainly wasn't going to say anything that might make him change his mind.

CHAPTER 6

Brick

BRICK COULDN'T BELIEVE THEY WERE headed to his room to fuck. When they'd originally made the vacation plans, he'd hoped, even daydreamed of it happening, but he'd certainly never expected it to work out so quickly, if not smoothly.

Watching Maxwell's ass as he followed him down the hall, Brick knew that it hadn't exactly been smooth.

Maxwell stopped in the doorway leading to the bedroom. "Brick, why don't you go grab a couple beers. I'll let mine trickle onto your stomach and suck it up off of you."

"What should I do with mine?"

Maxwell lightly pinched Brick's nipple. "You can pour it wherever you want me to suck next."

"Damn, man. You are making my dick so hard."

Brick caught his breath when Maxwell reached down to test it. "Mmhmm. I won't complain one bit if you pour some there."

Brick had no idea how he'd have the patience to not flip Maxwell onto his belly and fuck his ass. The hungry lips would be pleasant enough, but Brick would have bet money that neither of them would be finishing their beer.

"Get in that fucking bed. I'll be back in a minute."

Brick tried walking with a calm swagger to the kitchen. He didn't want to look too anxious. He wasn't some horny high schooler.

I'm a respectable firefighter. He's getting as much of a treat tonight as I am.

Saying the words didn't help him believe them.

They needed more than two weeks together, but there were no promises of anything after the all-too-short visit.

And there are only a few more hours left of today.

Pushed into action by the last thought, Brick tore through the drawers, looking for the bottle opener before realizing the tops twisted off. Just as he started back down the hall, his cell phone rang. He would have ignored any other ringtone, but "We Didn't Start the Fire" meant the station was calling and they only called from that number if there was an emergency.

51

"Shit."

Setting the bottles on the counter, he closed his eyes and answered the call. "Yeah."

"Hey." It was Marcus. "Sorry to call you on short notice. But there's a flu going around and we're down two people. You're first on the call-in list. I've got to follow protocol. You really shouldn't have answered, man."

Brick inhaled and exhaled slowly before answering. "Can I just quit?"

"I don't think you have the cojones for that," Marcus said. "Listen, I know you've got company and I'm truly sorry, but get your ass in here before you make me feel bad about myself for calling."

"Damn it. Fine. Can I have two hours?" Brick asked, glancing at the clock on the microwave.

Marcus laughed. "Who are you kidding? You won't need more than five minutes. But not tonight. Drew can't leave until you get here and they have tickets for a show tonight. You don't want his wife on your back."

"Hell, no. She'll stop sending in her pierogies. I'm coming. I'll be there in a few," Brick said.

"You don't have time for that. Just get driving."

Marcus ended the call just when Brick realized what his boss had implied. He was never going to live down Maxwell's visit.

Brick looked at the open beers, wishing he had already

been drinking all night. That would have been the only acceptable excuse for not coming in for overtime.

For one of the rare times in his life, Brick hated his job. He had some vacation days scheduled to start in a few days, but didn't have enough to take off the entire two weeks of Maxwell's visit.

When Brick returned to his bedroom, Maxwell looked up at him with a smile. He was naked, gorgeous, and slowly stroking his fat, tempting dick. It was nearly enough to bring Brick to tears.

"Sorry to start without you, but you got me all worked up out in the garage." Maxwell patted the spot next him. "Why don't you hop up and see if you can work your way in? Like Double Dutch."

Brick shook his head. "That was work. We've had some guys call in sick, so I have to go in."

His face turning serious, Maxwell nodded. "Duty calls. I get it. Rain check. Okay?"

Brick forced a smile. "Rain check. Keep that dick hard for me."

Maxwell started stroking again. "Don't worry, Brick. It doesn't take much effort to get hard when you are around. Go. Arm-wrestle some fires into submission and come back as soon as you can."

* * *

At the station, the guys wouldn't leave him alone for a second.

"I called Clay to talk about a fundraiser Ezra is trying to get him to start up," Marcus said. "Man, I hope they keep that down in their own station. Poor guy. When Ezzie gets an idea..." Marcus whistled to show how relieved he was to not have someone like that in his life. "Anyway, I heard you have a boy toy in town. How come we're the last to know? Is it because we're straight?"

"Speak for yourself," Levi said. Levi was the tallest firefighter Brick had ever met. Lean to the point of being skinny, but he never failed to catch the eye of any man or woman who crossed his path. He was one of the most fearless and loyal firefighters Brick knew. "I'm bi. Like Clay."

"Clay's not bi. He's gay. He's married to Ezra."

Brick sat silently in his chair letting the other guys argue, hoping they'd forget all about him and his guest.

A vein popped out on Levi's forehead. "Bi...just because he's with a man right now doesn't mean he's not bi."

Marcus loved riling up the easily excitable Levi. It made the nights pass more quickly when there was playful banter. "Sure it does. He's not sitting around thinking about eating pussy anymore. Ergo..."

"With all due respect...no, you're not due *any* respect," Levi said, leaning forward and banging his fist against the table. "Are you trying to say that if he'd married a woman, he'd be straight?"

Appearing confident that he was close to winning the argument, Marcus leaned back in his chair. "Absolutely."

"Okay. So when some chick is dumb enough to date you for a couple weeks, and you are monogamous until she dumps your ass, you are being straight, right?"

Marcus nodded, but the smile had left his face as he realized he wasn't sure where Levi was leading him. Brick knew, though, and could barely contain his excitement. Marcus deserved what was coming for making him come to work.

The rest of the room went silent, anxious for the punchline, too.

"So when you are in this perfectly straight, lovingly monogamous relationship, you only fantasize about her, right. You never imagine someone else while fucking or check out another ass when a hottie walks by?"

"Of course I do," Marcus said. "We all do."

"Yeah, I know," Levi grinned, ready to make his point. "When straight guys do it, it's always women. When gay guys do it, they always picture men. But us bisexuals. Well, we can fantasize about everyone."

Levi slowly looked at each man in the room in turn, finishing with Marcus.

Marcus swallowed, nervously, and fidgeted in his chair, which made Levi and Brick laugh in the otherwise silent room.

"Well, not everyone. You all are too ugly for me. But my point stands. Watch Clay sometime when a pretty waitress walks by. I bet every once in a while, one of them catches his eyes for a split second. He's married and bisexual. Not dead."

Now that Levi was done tormenting Marcus, Brick tried to look small and inconspicuous, hoping the group would turn to another topic.

Unfortunately, Marcus set his laser focus back on Brick. "So, who's this dude you're banging? I heard he was in the military."

"Sounds like you have a good source for your information. Why don't you go give them a call and I'll go take a nap."

Everything was still too soon with Maxwell. Despite the craziness earlier, there was something definitely real in his feelings toward the guy. He knew it probably wasn't anything more than lust yet, but he had an inkling that it could turn more serious.

Seeing the disappointed looks around the room, Brick decided to throw them a bone. The main reason they wanted to know any details was because they cared for Brick and knew exactly how hard it had been for him to find a man to date since coming out. They knew all about the disastrous date with David just before David and Quinn had met. And none of the others since had gone much better.

Brick stood and stretched. "I'm going to go try and get some sleep since I didn't have enough warning to prepare properly. I'm exhausted. It's been a busy day. I had my first orgasm five minutes after Maxwell showed up today."

He walked out of the room while all of their jaws were still dropped. Once the words were out of his mouth, he felt stupid and childish for gossiping, but still enjoyed the attention.

We firefighters are strange men.

Once he settled in his bunk, though, he couldn't sleep. He doubted he would ever sleep again because every time he closed his eyes, he saw Maxwell's naked body and wicked smile.

CHAPTER 7

Maxwell

MAXWELL FELT UNCOMFORTABLE IN THE crowded room full of strangers. Again.

What the hell is wrong with me?

The text from Brick announcing that a few friends were stopping by after work had seemed harmless enough. Plus, Maxwell had encouraged Brick to make sure they all got together again. But he still wasn't really prepared to spend time with eight loud firemen huddled around the small living room, screaming at the TV.

"Millions of dollars a year and he can't lay down a bunt!"

the oldest one of the group yelled. "Bunch of prima donnas. Put me out there for a fraction of that, and I'll bunt the ball."

"Sure you will, Marcus," Brick pretended to agree. "Only difference is that you'll be swinging for the fence but just barely get the ball past the pitcher."

Marcus threw a couch pillow at Brick, but hit Maxwell instead.

Reminding himself that getting hit by errant pillows on vacation was still better than having real bullets miss him back at work, Maxwell stayed calm, tossed the pillow back, and said, "It's a good thing you've got that bunting down, because you throw like shit."

As soon as the words left his mouth, Maxwell worried that he'd overstepped his boundaries. He didn't know these guys at all.

The laughter around the room quickly calmed his nerves. It was a familiar oasis. These guys reminded him of his Army buddies. Maxwell didn't hang out with the group back on base as much as the rest of the guys, but they were always there when they needed each other.

Still, Maxwell wished he weren't wedged in the middle of the couch. Wiggling out of his spot, he asked, "Anyone need a drink or some food?"

"Sit down, Maxwell," Brick said, quickly standing. "You're my guest. I'll take care of everything."

Whispering to Brick, Maxwell said, "I need to stretch my legs. But you can come with, if you really want to help." Maxwell grabbed both of Brick's hands and gave them a quick squeeze before talking loud enough for everyone else to hear. "I'm just grabbing a fresh round for everyone. It's the sixth inning, though, so I'm cutting you all off after this so you can drive home safely."

That should at least keep any of them from needing to crash on the couch.

Brick, and a chorus of boos from his friends, followed Maxwell into the kitchen. When he grabbed the refrigerator handle, Brick's huge hands started rubbing his shoulders, squeezing the tension away.

Maxwell leaned his head against the door. "Mmm. That feels great."

"Sorry to spring the guys on you. I forgot it was my week to host. You doing okay?"

No. I wish they'd all go away and leave us alone so we can fool around.

"Yeah. Like I said, I want to get to know them. It's just... they're so loud. It's not a problem. It's like that back on base, too. I'm just the outsider here, you know?"

"Yeah, I get it. Totally. I'll make sure we get more time with just the two of us for the rest of your trip."

Perfect. I'll make it worth your while, too, and then you'll definitely tell them to stay away while I'm in town.

Maxwell opened the refrigerator door and grabbed a case of beer. "Like I said, it's fine. Definitely don't let it ruin the game, okay? I've got the beer. Grab the chips. I think we're almost out in the other room."

"You're the best, man."

Brick pulled Maxwell close. Maxwell melted into what turned into a passionate kiss that reminded Maxwell of exactly what they were missing out on because of the guys in the other room.

While walking back to the living room, Maxwell prayed that the game didn't go into extra innings. He found it funny how much the tables had changed for him on this trip. He was normally the one telling the man or woman that he needed plenty of downtime during these trips to wander around wherever he was staying and do some exploring. It was how he handled it when things got intense. But so far, most of their interruptions had been Brick's fault. Maxwell had been in town longer than twenty-four hours and hadn't gotten laid once.

Am I losing my touch?

He peeked at his reflection in the microwave door, and swore that the worry lines on the corners of his eyes hadn't gotten any longer in the last year.

"Beer!" the tall guy—*is he Levi?*—called from the other room.

The rest echoed their request.

Maxwell forced a smile and hurried to join them.

The empty spot on the couch had closed up, so he set the beer on the coffee table and stood against the wall.

"Come sit down. We'll make room," Brick offered.

Maxwell waved off the invitation. "It's fine. I might head out and take a few pictures if you don't mind."

"Oh, shit," Marcus interrupted. "That reminds me of Ezra's plan. Check this out. He wants to get Clay's station to do one of those sexy firemen calendars for some charity. Can you imagine anyone buying a calendar with all those ugly dudes?"

Levi laughed and said, "Yeah, but it's not like we'd be much better. I mean, I'm pretty. And Brick ain't bad. But the rest of you? I guess maybe if you Photoshopped off your heads...and stomachs...and, well, and the rest of you."

Marcus raised his two middle fingers at Levi. "You're not exactly wrong, though." He flexed his arms. "You're way off base with me, but the rest of these guys are real dogs. Woof."

After the room quieted from everyone barking, Maxwell said, "What you guys should do is combine stations. You guys all basically cover the area up and down this river, right? I keep forgetting. What's it called?"

"The Fox River." Brick said.

"Yeah, right. We could gather up all the male firefighters worth being in the calendar and call it Firefighters on the Fox or something stupid like that," Levi offered.

"Firefighters on the Fox," one of the men said. "My wife would buy the hell out of that."

"Why buy it when we bring it right to her bedroom whenever you're working?" Marcus said, earning laughs and more taunts directed at the older guy.

Marcus quieted the room. Based on how quickly they followed his lead, Maxwell figured he must be in charge. "That's a really solid idea, Max...sorry, Maxwell. We just have one problem. Ezra told us what the photos would cost. We don't have the budget for that."

Maxwell realized that he'd accidentally stepped into his own trap, and there was no way out but pushing all the way through. "I can take them. I might already have one that we can use of Brick."

The room erupted into oohs and ahhs and one, "Show me!"

Brick, throwing Maxwell a lifeline, asked, "Are you sure about that? You're supposed to be on vacation."

Tell me about it. A vacation where I'm supposed to be banging a hot fireman, not hanging out with his friends.

Despite his private thoughts, he still found himself saying, "You kidding? It sounds great."

The strange thing was that Maxwell wasn't even lying. Taking their photos *did* promise to be great fun, and the calendar was for charity.

It'll feel good to do something good for people that doesn't involve getting shot at by bad guys.

After gathering all their attention with the calendar,

Maxwell was uncertain whether it would be okay to leave. But Brick interrupted a question from Levi by saying, "Hey, I'm trying to watch a game here. Maxwell, have fun with the photos. Hurry back," and blowing him a kiss.

The guys all said a loud, "Aww." But other than that, Maxwell was quickly ignored, which allowed him to get outside for a walk.

CHAPTER 8

Brick

B RICK STRETCHED HIMSELF AWAKE, AND frowned when he noticed it was almost dinner time. The last thing he wanted was to waste these two weeks with Maxwell and he was already feeling like it was passing too quickly with them doing too little together.

I hope he didn't get lost.

Brick closed his eyes and lay back down on the couch, wondering how long he'd give Maxwell before starting to search for him. He didn't stay on the couch long, though. When he heard a click from across the room, he jumped up and noticed that

Maxwell was standing in the doorway to the kitchen snapping pictures of him sleeping.

"Good evening, sleepyhead," Maxwell said in a happy voice. "You don't plan to sleep away my entire vacation do you?"

"Of course not," Brick mumbled, realizing that he was the main reason they hadn't been spending time together.

After all, he'd been the one who'd answered the phone, knowing it was a call for overtime. He'd taken Maxwell to Clay and Ezra's. And he'd invited the guys from work over for the baseball game. To top it off, he'd been the one sleeping the afternoon away during the first free time they *did* have together.

Shaking his head to clear out the cobwebs, he said, "Sorry. Let's go out. You and me. Like a real date."

"You sure?" Maxwell asked, looking down the hallway toward the bedrooms. "We could just have some pizza delivered and eat it in the privacy of your bed, naked."

As tempting as the thought of getting Maxwell into his bed was, it would be strange to do it without going out first.

That's how it normally goes, right? Dinner, walk around town, and then come home to fuck?

Brick didn't have enough experience dating men to know what was normal, so he had to rely on what he'd learned from watching his friends. What they'd done when they'd first met was not healthy, and even a decent fling needed something more than just sex and pizza. Not that either was ever a bad thing, but he wanted more with Maxwell.

"How about we go for a walk?" Brick countered. "Get to know each other a little more, and then go out for pizza, and then go to the movie theater. Then we can come home and see where the evening takes us."

That sounded mature enough that Brick wouldn't feel too dirty about sex afterward, but still implied that Brick was totally suggesting they should fuck. He puffed out his chest a little bit at his bold plan.

"Most of that sounds okay, but how about this little compromise?" Maxwell said, still leaning against the wall.

Shit. This is where he asks me to take him to an expensive restaurant and I spend the night feeling like a John.

Brick felt vulnerable standing in the middle of the room. He put his hands in his front pockets and then moved them to the back ones, and shifted his weight from side to side.

Maxwell held up his index finger. "Walk."

Brick's ears perked up when Maxwell's plan started with something as simple, and cheap, as a walk.

He held up another finger. "Pizza."

This is the same plan.

The dramatic pauses made Brick's body tingle. Maxwell flashed a smile that said he knew exactly the effect he was having. Brick was ready for release when Maxwell raised his third finger.

"Fuck."

Brick nodded. "Hell, yes! Movies are entirely overrated."

"Unless you want to go to a theater, watch some shit movie that no one else will see, and fuck in the back row. But that sounds like a future date. Something for when we get bored of the bedroom."

Suddenly, Brick wasn't so sure that movies were overrated at all. Maxwell had effortlessly made Brick's plan sound lame as hell, tossing it to the side to cut to the important bits, and had then gone and turned Brick's tame movie theater suggestion into something right out of a porno.

Who is this guy?

Brick had never wanted to go to the theater so badly before. His dick got hard just thinking about Maxwell sliding his pants down to his ankles and sitting on Brick's lap in the darkness of an empty theater.

I'll never make it through a meal in a restaurant at this rate. I won't even make it out of the house for a walk without getting arrested for indecency.

Brick shook his head, hoping that he looked like a composed negotiator. "Order pizza delivered and fuck. Forget the rest."

He wanted to rush forward, pin Maxwell against the wall to kiss him, and forget all about the pizza.

Maxwell set his camera on the kitchen counter. "Walk. Pizza at home. Fuck. I deserve some kind of a proper date, I think. I am a gentleman, you know." Maxwell lowered his eyes to Brick's crotch. "You'll need to do something to hide that monster, though. You don't want to scare away anyone we meet along the riverwalk."

Brick tried to think about baseball, his grandma, even the Bible, but nothing was helping with his raging erection. Reaching into his pants, he adjusted himself to hide it as well as possible.

"Come on," Brick said. "Let's get this walk over with. Will just around the block be enough?"

When Maxwell picked up his camera, Brick knew that Maxwell's idea of a walk was going to take much longer than Brick had hoped. He bet Maxwell would make it take exactly as long as it took to convince him that Brick was entirely at his mercy.

They would fuck when Maxwell was ready and not a second earlier.

Somehow, that frustration turned Brick on even more.

"I heard there's a windmill around here somewhere," he held the camera up toward Brick. "Let's go check it out and take some pictures. Windmills and penis pictures sound sexy."

Brick longed to throw Maxwell over his shoulder, carry him to bed for a good fucking, and then do whatever Maxwell wanted afterward, but if he tried, Maxwell would probably do some badass Army commando shit, and make Brick submit. Instead he nodded his agreement, planning to look for a moment when he might be able to turn the tables later.

The two men hurried outside, neither saying anything

until they had reached the bike path along the edge of the river.

Maxwell finally broke the silence. "How far is it to the windmill?"

Brick shrugged. "I'm not really sure. It's just kind of down there. I see it as I pass when I go jogging once in a while, but don't really see it, you know?"

"Completely," Maxwell agreed. "That's why I love photography. It forces me to slow down and pay attention to the places I visit."

"Do you have a lot of pictures of Idaho?" Brick asked, stepping toward the windmill.

"No. I want to go there someday and do some fly fishing and get some pictures of that."

What the hell?

Brick was certain that Maxwell had said he was from Idaho earlier. Not just fairly certain, either. One hundred percent certain. Brick had even mentioned wanting to see buffalo.

Weird. Why would he have lied about that?

The obvious answer hit Brick immediately.

He's lying because he doesn't want me to get to know him for real. He's here for two weeks and then he'll be gone forever, and he thinks that the less I know, the better.

Brick took a moment to decide how that made him feel. A long-term relationship between them *would* be stupid and probably doomed to failure. Maxwell couldn't quit his job or even transfer somewhere close to Brick. And Brick couldn't follow him to places like Afghanistan.

A fling really was the best of all worlds. Fun while they were together. Fun memories when they were apart. And no sad breakups in the future.

Maybe all of this will help give me the confidence I need to land my forever man after Maxwell heads back.

If Brick decided he was okay not pushing for anything more than a fling, it didn't really matter what kind of lies Maxwell made up as long as they didn't impact their brief time together.

Nodding his head as if to convince himself of his decision, he changed the subject. "When you take pictures of my dick later, do you think black and white or color will be the best?"

Maxwell laughed. He sounded relieved, as if he'd realized his own lie after saying it and had worried that Brick was going to call him out on it. "Black and white all the way. Anything that big looks amazing in black and white. Such great shadows."

Brick bumped against Maxwell, shoving him sideways as they walked. "I've seen yours, too, man. That's totally a black and white spectacle. You'll have to let me take a few pictures of you later."

Maxwell looked up at Brick's face. His eyes danced around,

71

looking for something before nodding. "Okay. If you want. I normally don't let people take pictures of me, but I think I can trust you."

Brick couldn't help but wonder how many people Maxwell had told that exact lie to in the past.

CHAPTER 9

Maxwell

AXWELL WAS SURE HE'D SCREWED everything up with the Idaho comment. But either Brick hadn't caught the mix-up or didn't care. Either way, it didn't seem like it was going to ruin their first moment alone together in too long.

The rain hit before they could even see the windmill through the dense trees along the side of the river. It quickly turned into a downpour.

"Your camera!" Brick screamed over the thunder rumbling in the distance.

"It's fine!" Maxwell yelled back. "The bag's waterproof. Should we go back home, though?"

"I think the windmill is just around the corner. It'll take less time to get there. I think it has a ledge or balcony that we can hide under and wait out the worst of it."

Maxwell followed Brick when he started jogging down the path. After a bend in the road, the windmill appeared out of nowhere in front of them on the left.

The old, rickety windmill had long since passed beyond cute and quaint. Maxwell wondered if it was even smart to take shelter from the storm that was still building momentum.

The windmill was attached to the top of a three-story building that was entirely out of place along the edge of the river. It almost looked like they'd attached the arms of the windmill to a lighthouse, not that a lighthouse would have made any better sense.

Brick was panting with his hands on his knees near the door beneath the second-floor balcony that looked newer than the rest of the building.

When Brick looked up at Maxwell, he said between breaths, "You're not even breathing hard...that's ridiculous."

Doing his best to shake off any lingering paranoia about what he'd said earlier, he tried to regain his swagger. "PT every day. Twice on Sundays. You're going to need to do more than that to make me short of breath. I have faith that you'll figure out something, though."

Brick's smile showed that Maxwell was headed in the right direction again.

Their clothes were drenched. It felt like they'd fallen into the river rather than just getting caught in the rain. Maxwell stared at Brick's t-shirt. It had gone slightly translucent from the rain and was clinging to his skin, allowing Maxwell to see Brick's nipples and the curves of his chest. Water dripped from the end of Brick's nose, from his ears, and from his chin.

The only thing sexier than Brick was a wet Brick.

Maxwell needed him no matter what the storm threatened to do.

Swinging his camera bag onto his back, he stepped forward to press his body against Brick's. A bolt of lightning briefly brightened the dark sky when the two men kissed. Brick matched Maxwell's hunger as their tongues explored each other.

The electricity in the air couldn't hold a candle to what Brick was doing to Maxwell. If Maxwell's hair wasn't shaved so short, the lightning might have made it stand on end, but with just his mouth, Brick was having no trouble making Maxwell's cock stand at attention.

They continued kissing until the thunder shook the evening.

Maxwell pushed against Brick's chest to break away and say, "Two miles."

Brick looked confused. "What are you talking about?"

Feeling proud of himself for being able to teach Brick something, Maxwell pointed up at the sky. "The lightning. It's two miles away. Ten seconds between the lightning and the thunder. Two miles. You didn't know that?"

"Oh, yeah. I knew that. I didn't know I was such a boring kisser that you could count the thunder during it, though."

It really did sound bad when Brick said it out loud, but he sounded more amused than anything. Maxwell was happy to hear the playful tone in his voice. "Yeah, well, I have to do something to pass the time."

"Let me try again and see if I can do better." Brick licked his own lips in preparation.

Maxwell had been counting lightning since he was a kid. Growing up on the plains of Nebraska, storms had scared the hell out of him as a kid. His mom has taught him the trick to help him calm down. Realizing how far away the lightning really had been was a relief, since they were almost always way further away than they sounded.

He didn't need to let Brick know how automatic the calculation was for him, though. "I don't know. I was thinking about doing one of those math problems where a train leaves westbound for Chicago traveling—"

Maxwell didn't get a chance to finish. Brick pushed him up against the door while leaning in for what promised to be an even more powerful kiss. Based on the storm raging across

Brick's face, there was no safe place to hide from what he was planning to unleash.

The kiss never struck, though. When Maxwell's body hit the door, it swung open and the two tumbled inside, falling to the floor, and laughing as they hit the ground.

Brick recovered first and straddled Maxwell's body, pinning him to the floor. Maxwell knew several ways to get his body out from under the much larger man, but couldn't think of a single reason to use any of them. Maxwell was perfectly happy right where he was for a little while.

The thought tried to bother him. He didn't like being anywhere for any real amount of time. But while trapped under Brick, he just wished there'd be more time for them to be together. In fact at that moment, Brick's plain little house in the suburbs sounded more exciting than any mansion in San Diego.

What the hell? The suburbs?

The answer was a resounding yes, as long as he was there with Brick.

He filed that thought away. Something to ponder on a sunny day. The stormy weather called for fucking.

Pretending to buck his hips helplessly against Brick, he said, "Now that you've captured me, what are you planning to do with me?"

"You fucking liar," Brick said.

Maxwell nearly panicked. Was this how Brick was going to call him out about lying about where he was from? Being trapped under the sexy fireman was fine if they were having fun, but the accusation shook him to the core until he realized that Brick was still smiling.

"I don't believe that I've captured you at all. How hard would it be for you to escape?"

Brick shifted his weight, stabilizing himself for the move he expected from Maxwell.

"The easy way would break your arm. The other two ways would take a little more work, but we wouldn't have to spend the night in the hospital. But we can pretend you have me pinned for real...for tonight. I don't want to waste any time in a hospital. I'd rather spend time in your mouth."

"Prepare to have your mind blown. Nobody knows how to handle a good hose better than a fireman."

Maxwell groaned, but slid his hands up inside the bottom of Brick's shirt, hoping he'd get the hint and pull it off. The sooner they both got undressed, the quicker they could get what they really wanted.

Brick's flirting was silly and awkward, but earnest enough that it was making Maxwell fall even harder for the big lug after years of pushing everyone away. Maxwell practically growled in wild abandon when Brick started pulling his shirt up over his head.

But they both froze when they heard a woman laugh.

Brick scrambled off Maxwell and they both hurried to their feet.

"Who's there?" Maxwell called out. "We're not here to hurt you, we were just coming in from the storm."

"It sounds like you were just getting ready to come from what I can tell," a familiar voice said. "Did you even notice the rain?"

"Who are you?" Brick asked, squinting his eyes.

"Relax," Maxwell said, putting his hand against Brick's forearm to keep him from doing something rash and macho. "It's just my friend, Nicole."

She stepped out from behind a stack of boxes. "Sorry. I've been hanging out in here for a few hours. I wouldn't have interrupted you, but..." her voice went an octave deeper. "'Nobody knows how to handle a good hose better than a fireman.'" She giggled and returned to using her normal voice. "That was just too funny. It's a shame, really, because it was looking to be a great show. You can go back to it if you want. Don't mind me."

Brick turned toward Maxwell. "You know her?"

"Yeah. She helped me out when I got to town. When you didn't show up, she's the one that drove me to your place." Maxwell gave Nicole a quick hug. "You remember what happened then. You really should thank her for giving me that ride."

Brick's head swung back and forth between Maxwell and Nicole.

Nicole held her hands apart in front of her and then moved them toward each other. "Now kiss?"

"Jesus," Brick said, moving toward the door.

Maxwell, trying to stifle a laugh, said, "Sorry, Brick," while wondering what he was apologizing for. He hadn't done anything. It was just bad luck that she'd taken shelter in the same building as them. "It sure does seem hard for us to get laid, doesn't it?"

Nicole squeaked. "Oh no. Not that. If I would have known you were coming here to fuck or make love or whatever you two guys like to do, I would have laid down roses for you two to roll around on to help set the mood."

When Brick backed out the door, Maxwell noticed that rain had already mostly stopped.

"So that's your boyfriend?" Nicole asked when they were alone.

"Yeah. He's a good guy," Maxwell answered, still looking out the door, hoping Brick would reconsider and return so they could hold hands while they walked home together.

"You going to be okay?" Nicole asked, moving behind Maxwell and wrapping him in a hug. "You look lost in space."

"Yeah. I'll be fine." Maxwell patted her arms, grateful for any friend at the moment. "It's just too bad I'll only be here for a couple weeks since something keeps coming up with us at the worst times. There are just so many things that I want to do with him and we're going to run out of time."

"You can always come back again the next time you have leave. Hell, you can even come back for good when you retire."

"I know, but that's just not what I do."

Maxwell gently broke free of her grasp and headed after Brick.

CHAPTER 10

Brick

*W*HY IS GETTING LAID SO *hard?*

As Brick walked back toward his house, he almost wished Maxwell didn't make him horny so easily. As much as he enjoyed hanging around the guy, he was growing frustrated with their inability to find an opportunity to fuck. It was worse to keep getting so close and having it never come to fruition.

And where the hell had that girl come from? As much as he wanted to get laid, the thought of that creepy woman sneaking up on them was probably going to haunt his dreams for a while.

If I hadn't said that embarrassingly corny line, she probably would have watched the whole thing. I can't even have a fling the right way.

Brick knew that if he walked home, Maxwell would show up soon enough and they'd talk. Everything would sound great, and they would probably head to the bedroom after.

Isn't that what you want?

Somehow even that wasn't good enough.

Brick knew he'd go home soon enough, and they'd finally get their chance in bed. He wanted the sex, but he wanted more, too. And with less than two weeks remaining, he struggled to figure out exactly how he wanted to spend that time with Maxwell.

I need more time to think.

Instead of turning toward his house, he headed further down the riverwalk and dove into the first bar he came across, hoping the noise there would silence the chaos in his brain. He would take a few minutes to clear his head and calm down from being spooked in the windmill.

He sat at the bar and ordered a beer without bothering to look around and acknowledge anyone but the bartender. Brick had just finished his first sip, and turned to see what game might be on TV when David called his name.

David patted him on the back as he sat down next to him and ordered a drink of his own.

"What are you doing up here in my neck of the woods?" Brick asked.

"Just doing a little shopping. Looking for a little gift for Quinn."

Both men stared at their drinks and fell silent. Brick considered chugging his and finding an excuse to leave. He certainly didn't want to talk to David about any of it. David was blissfully in love with Quinn and had known he was almost immediately. He wouldn't understand Brick's confusion.

Before Brick had the chance to stand up, David said. "So, I'm glad I bumped into you. I have a question. I know that I'm supposed to be getting photographed for this calendar, but I can't help thinking that no one is going to want to see me on their wall for a whole month."

Brick, still feeling a little crabby that David had interrupted his solitude, said, "Okay? You said you had a question?"

Brick felt horrible when his friend's eyes darted from his beer up to Brick's face and back. He clearly was nervous about whatever he was trying to say.

"Sorry," Brick said with a sigh. "But you can't really be worried about the calendar, can you? You're a gorgeous man and you know it." A smile broke out on David's face, making Brick wonder if it was possible that he *didn't* know. "There's a reason you had me so flustered on that blind date we had back before you met Quinn. He's a lucky man to have you, and the people that buy the calendar will be lucky to have you on their wall for whatever month you get. I bet it will be one with thirty-one days, though."

Brick felt a million times better when David blushed at the compliment.

"Thanks," David said before taking a sip of his drink. "I'll still be nervous, I guess, but I won't back out of doing it."

"You better not. It's for charity. Just have fun with it. How often do guys like us get a chance for something crazy like this? It'll make some great memories no matter how it goes."

David clinked his bottle against Brick's. "Speaking of, how are things with the boyfriend?"

Brick groaned. "Complicated."

David arched his eyebrows, questioningly, but didn't press the issue further.

Brick surprised himself by continuing. "I really like Maxwell. Like I told you guys the other day, we started out by fooling around right when he came to town, which was pretty awesome."

Brick rubbed the condensation from one side of his bottle while gathering his thoughts. "That was the original plan, after all. Hot and sweaty fun times. But then we were about to, well, you know, the other day when I got called in for overtime. And just a little bit ago, we were fooling around in the windmill, and got interrupted by this woman who had been hiding out in there."

Brick paused to finish the last of his drink, and flagged down the bartender for another.

"It just never seems to work out. And when I'm around

him, he's just a really fun guy...outside of just the sex...that we're not having anyway. Fuck. Back when we were emailing, we used to have these great conversations about everything and nothing. Now that he's here, I'm finding myself wishing we had more than two weeks, but we don't. He'll be gone, and won't be coming back, I'm sure, and I'll be back to being all alone. So what's the point in doing anything now and getting too attached?"

David nodded and fiddled with his drink. "That's a tough one. Just because you guys only agreed to two weeks doesn't mean it can't turn into more later on, though. Don't forget, Quinn and I originally planned on breaking up after New Year's, and look where we are now."

Brick sighed. He wanted to believe there could be something more, but he knew being realistic would protect him from getting hurt later.

"That's not even a fair comparison, though," Brick argued, trying not to sound too annoyed. "You guys were both living here from the start. Maxwell doesn't live here and he doesn't have any reason to come back after we've had our fun. Once he's gone, that'll be it."

David patted Brick's shoulder and gave it a little squeeze. "Sorry you're going through all of that. You want my opinion?" Without waiting for a reply, he continued. "It sounds like you just need to dive into this fling. A fling is better than not having anything, right? Like you said about me and the calendar. It'll be an experience."

"I was just telling myself that before you showed up. I'm just worried that I'll get too attached, and when he gets back on that plane to leave, I'll end up devastated."

"Sure, you'll probably cry and be sad for a little while. But all of your friends will be here for you. We're not going anywhere. And someone else great will come along soon enough. I'll make you a deal. I'll embrace the calendar, if you embrace the sexy soldier waiting for you to come home and give him a kiss."

Brick laughed. He really did want to believe...maybe not even believe, but just do it anyway. It would certainly be easier than spending the next two weeks running away from the guy staying at his place. "Deal. I'll embrace my situation and laugh at you while you worry about what to do with your hands during the pictures."

The two laughed and turned their attention to the baseball game that was showing on the television behind the bar. The Cubs were down by a run in the ninth inning.

"So, what are you looking to buy Quinn?" Brick asked.

"No idea. Just something. He's been a little stressed about going back to work this fall so I thought a little gift might make him a little happier at least. Any ideas?"

"Yeah, actually. There's an antique shop down on the river.

They have a couple things he might like. Last time I was there, they had some of those card catalogs like libraries used to have."

David gave Brick a questioning look.

"Teachers love that kind of thing. They also had an old-fashioned wooden desk that I bet he'd like, too."

"Ah, yeah. That does sound up his alley. Brian would probably love playing on it, too. I'll have to check it out. What were you doing at an antique shop, though?"

"Well, just walking around and...window shopping...supporting local—"

David laughed. "The owner's cute?"

"Yeah," Brick admitted, embarrassed that he'd been that easy to read. "He is if you like the hot, college professor look."

David raised his glass to Brick. Brick raised his back and finished it off.

Up on the television, the Cubs' batter connected on a curve ball, launching it high toward the ivy-covered wall in center field. The bar got silent, hoping for a home run. The center fielder backpedaled and jumped at the last second, snagging the ball just before it could clear the wall for a home run. The game ended with Chicago losing by one run.

Brick and David joined the collective groan that erupted in the bar. Since winning the World Series the previous fall, Chicago fans expected wins every game, but that was proving more difficult than anyone could have predicted.

"I hope they get out of this scoring slump soon," Brick said.

"I'm sure they will. They're probably just overthinking things and putting too much pressure on themselves." David started to open his mouth again, but Brick quickly interrupted him.

"Yeah, yeah. I get it. I'm overthinking things and putting too much pressure on what's happening with Maxwell. I just need to get out there and swing the bat, right?"

David nodded and patted Brick on the shoulder. "Swing for the fences, big guy. Okay. I have to get out of here. Good luck with Maxwell."

"Thanks. Thanks for the pep talk, too." When David reached for his wallet, Brick added, "I'll even pay for your drinks."

"I would have ordered something good if I'd known."

"If you had, I wouldn't have paid. Seriously, though. Thanks for the chat. I'll have to get together with you and Quinn sometime for dinner."

"Sure, but it better not be until your soldier has returned to duty. Other than work, you better not get out of bed until then."

Brick promised to do his best as they went their separate ways.

CHAPTER 11

Maxwell

MAXWELL QUICKLY GREW NERVOUS WHEN he walked into the house and Brick wasn't there. He couldn't really afford a hotel if Brick decided to kick him out, and without really knowing what he was doing wrong, Maxwell didn't know what he could do to make the situation any better.

None of his trips had ever been this difficult before, which he thought was strange because he hadn't been as attracted to any of his previous partners nearly as much as Brick. The guy's body was driving Maxwell insane, but he couldn't seem to get his hands on it long enough to have any fun.

If my balls get any more blue, I'm going to have to name them after Smurfs.

He flopped onto the couch and turned on the end of one baseball game and started to watch the next while waiting for Brick to return. Fortunately, he only had to worry for about a half-hour before the door banged open, sending Maxwell scrambling to his feet.

"Maxwell, are you here?" Brick called from the entryway.

Hearing Brick's deep bass voice made Maxwell's knees go weak. It was a voice of command and authority. Maxwell was normally the one to take the initiative with his vacation partners, but all he could think of when he was around Brick was how insanely hot it would be for Brick to use his strength and pin Maxwell against a wall or a mattress and take what he needed.

He felt his face get warm as he once again pictured himself trapped beneath Brick's body, his own chest pressed against the cool sheets on Brick's bed. They'd come so close out in the windmill.

We have to figure out how to get this visit back on track.

"Yeah. Are you okay?" Maxwell asked.

"I am now." When Brick joined Maxwell in the TV room, he had a huge grin on his face. "I bumped into a friend and… everything is great now. That is as long as you're still okay."

Maxwell nodded quickly. His dick rose in anticipation when he heard the excitement in Brick's voice.

"Great," Brick said. "Listen, we can sit around and talk through all of this or we can just go to my room and you can let me give you that blowjob I promised you earlier."

Maxwell couldn't believe his ears. Brick sounded completely confident and ready to go. "You're okay with that? Just us having fun and keeping it casual?"

"Not really." Brick forced a brief smile. "I'll be bummed when it has to end, but I'm not interested in missing out on what we *can* have now just because of that."

Maxwell let out a breath he'd been holding in. Everything was back on track.

"So where do we go from here?" Maxwell asked, his heart pounding in his chest, hoping Brick would continue taking the lead. He could barely resist begging him to take the next step, but that would defeat the purpose of having Brick be in charge.

"Well, like I mentioned earlier, we could go to my room."

Maxwell could hear the hesitation in Brick's voice. Brick was waiting for permission.

"Sure. We could do that. Whatever you want, Brick." Maxwell hoped he sounded casual.

"Or we could just...right here on the couch." Brick dropped his eyes to the floor, avoiding Maxwell.

"Yep," Maxwell said, keeping his voice perky and inviting. "We could do that, too."

Brick finally looked up into Maxwell's eyes, clearly trying

to make an important decision. Maxwell would help him with that decision but only if Brick told him to.

"You're playing games with me, aren't you?" Brick finally asked.

"No. Not really. I'll happily do whatever you ask, Brick. *That* is exactly what I want to do."

"Pull out your dick." The command and authority was back in full force.

Maxwell hesitated, not sure he had heard Brick correctly. When Maxwell didn't move, Brick repeated the command with a little more growl in his voice.

Damn. He sounds sexy when he does that.

Not wanting to disobey the order that he was so desperate for anyway, Maxwell unbuttoned his pants, tugged down the zipper, and pulled his already-hard dick from his underwear.

"Like this?"

Brick nodded and frowned at the same time. "But do it when I tell you the first time from now on."

"Yes, sir." The words felt silly until Maxwell realized that he meant them. Deep down, he needed someone to tell him what to do for once. He was tired of always feeling the pressure to figure out other people's desires.

"Stroke your dick."

Maxwell instantly grabbed ahold and slowly started stroking. "Am I doing it right, Brick?"

"Yes. Get it good and hard so it's nice and ready for me."

"Jesus, man. If it gets any harder, I'll explode."

"Perfect. Now get on your knees and suck my dick."

Maxwell, realizing that he wasn't going to get his quick-and-easy release, forced himself to suppress his groan of frustration. He was excited enough to get ahold of Brick's big dick, and any complaining might lead to a punishment.

He'd done that to partners in the past—gotten them right to the point of being ready to come and then made them stop. And if they complained, then they had to wait until the next day.

I'm not going to wait until tomorrow.

He dropped to his knees and opened his mouth, hoping he looked tantalizing.

"Should I crawl to you or wait here for you to shove your dick into my mouth?"

Brick didn't answer until he had slowly and deliberately removed his own clothes, leaving himself standing naked in front of Maxwell with a dick that was rapidly getting harder.

Finally, he said the words Maxwell needed to hear. "Crawl over to me."

The rough carpet scratched at Maxwell's knees as he moved slowly across the floor. He kept his eyes aimed at Brick the entire way, lost in the hunger on his face.

When Maxwell reached Brick, he was impossibly large,

towering over him. His massive dick was right at mouth level. Maxwell was more than ready to take it into his mouth, but knew he was supposed to get permission first. He struggled with that thought for a moment. Always fiercely independent and capable of having people do what he wanted them to do, it was confusing to be on the other end of that power play.

Confusing and exciting.

Following Brick's guidance might introduce Maxwell to new experiences and push his boundaries into directions that he wouldn't have the courage to explore on his own, but it would certainly make it harder for Maxwell when he had to leave.

I'll cross that bridge some other day.

"What do you want, Brick?"

Brick's answer was wordless. He grabbed Maxwell by the back of the head, and thrust his dick into Maxwell's mouth.

Maxwell's eyes shot wide open feeling the fullness in his mouth. There was no way he could handle it all, but Brick didn't slow down to give Maxwell time to decide what to do about it. When he felt Brick against the back of his throat, Maxwell moved his own head back to halt the invasion, giving himself time to regroup and figure out how to win the battle.

Quickly realizing that he needed to use his hands, too, he wrapped them both around the warm cock, delighting at its girth.

Brick refused to give Maxwell time to adjust, though. His desires were clearly too strong. With a grunt, he started thrusting urgently.

Holding on like his life depended on it, Maxwell was able to manage Brick's needs. He latched his lips on tightly and found ways to tease Brick with his tongue.

Brick seemed to like the tongue play. He slowed, allowing Maxwell a better chance to flick his tongue against Brick's slippery, wet tip. Maxwell tasted the salty pre-cum and wanted more.

With his free hand, he cupped Brick's testicles, deciding that he approved of Brick waxing more than just his chest. Brick moaned and spread his legs.

Maxwell wondered what it must feel like to have someone rubbing the smooth skin, but doubted he'd ever be able to survive the waxing session to have it done to himself.

He let his fingers slide back further between Brick's legs, and circle his ass.

Worrying that he might be taking things too far, Maxwell took a breath and asked, "Is that okay?"

Brick moaned his consent.

If they'd had lube, Maxwell would have penetrated and massaged Brick's prostate, but had to satisfy himself with just circling what he knew were the sensitive nerves while continuing to suck Brick's dick.

"Dude, that's just too much." Brick said with his eyes closed and a look of pleasure on his face. When Maxwell moved his finger away, Brick added, "Don't you dare stop. It's a good too much. I want to come in your mouth so badly."

While Maxwell was never shy to suck his partners' dicks, he rarely let them finish in his mouth, but when he heard Brick's wish, he immediately wanted to swallow Brick's load and make him happy.

"Me, too," he managed to mumble with the dick still in his mouth.

Practically glowing while watching the focused expression on Brick's face, Maxwell helped him along by aggressively pumping his dick and continuing to tease his ass.

The two men worked in perfect unison for several more minutes. Maxwell hoped he was doing as much as he could to make it pleasurable for Brick. Such an intimate connection was rare for Maxwell and, even as it was happening, he was having trouble deciding what it meant.

The only thing that he could agree with himself about was that it was a shame he would be leaving in less than two weeks.

I seem to be thinking that a lot, but there's absolutely nothing I can do about it.

Rather than letting his thoughts turn dark, he reminded himself to embrace their mantra of enjoying the time they were going to have together for as long as it lasted.

Brick's breathing grew louder, reminding Maxwell of his duty. He doubled the speed of his bobbing head and hands until he felt Brick pull roughly on his hair, and saw his legs lock in place, giving Maxwell the only warning he would get before the warm load shot deep against the back of his throat.

Brick filled his mouth as quickly as Maxwell could swallow. Just when he started worrying that he wasn't going to make it, Brick finally stopped as his body relaxed.

Maxwell let his lips ride up and down a few more times before Brick begged him to stop and pushed him away, laughing. Despite the orgasm, Brick was still rock hard.

"That was amazing, man," he said. "Absolutely top notch."

Maxwell laughed and pushed Brick away. "You sound drunk. Don't talk anymore," he said playfully.

"Are you sure? I was just about to ask what you wanted me to do for you."

Maxwell stood up quickly and clapped his hands together. "Well, now. That changes everything. Carry on."

"Well, I was just thinking that you were a good soldier and did every little thing that I asked for and that I wouldn't be a good civil servant if I wasn't willing to return the favor. And I figured that with you being military, and clearly very good at taking orders, that it might be fun to have you give the orders for a little bit."

Maxwell nodded. "Okay. But you're stretching that military thing quite a bit."

"I'll do that, too, if you want me too."

Maxwell cocked his head. It took a second for him to

realize that Brick was talking dirty. When he did, Maxwell groaned dramatically.

"Okay," Maxwell said with his hands on his hips, trying to ignore how silly he felt with his erection bouncing freely. "First order is that you don't speak until told to speak. That should minimize the painful banter."

Brick opened his mouth to protest, but snapped it shut when Maxwell scowled and pointed a warning finger in his direction.

"Good," Maxwell continued, a plan forming in his head. "Are you really willing to do anything for me?"

"Absolutely, Officer."

"I'm just a Sergeant, but that's great. What I want might have been better for you before you came, but you're just going to have to press through and try to hold on to make me happy. Do you think you can do that for me?"

Brick puffed out his chest. "I can do whatever you need. Put me to the test."

Maxwell was just barely able to stop himself from laughing at the display. "Okay there, hotshot. Let's go to your bedroom."

Maxwell slapped Brick's butt when he thought Brick was strolling a little too slowly. Brick immediately picked up the pace.

As they walked through the bedroom door, Maxwell said, "Okay. On your back on the bed, Mister."

When Brick lay down, Maxwell noticed that Brick's

erection still hadn't faded one bit. Pointing at the swollen dick, Maxwell said, "Not that I'm complaining, but how is that even possible, man?"

Brick shook his head, and absentmindedly stroked himself. "I have no idea. What's next?"

"You lay there with your hands behind your head and don't move until I tell you."

Maxwell quickly embraced his normal commanding presence in bed, and Brick just as quickly complied. His chest looked even larger when he spread his arms and put his hands behind his head. "Like this?"

"Damn, man. That's quite a chest."

"Thanks. I came in third place—"

"We can talk about that some other time."

While wondering at both of their abilities to so quickly switch roles, Maxwell climbed up onto the bed and settled over Brick's legs. He shifted his hips until their dicks just about touched, and wrapped his fingers around the tip of his own dick and spread the pre-cum over the rest of it, getting himself nice and slick. He would have preferred lube, but wasn't nearly patient enough to track down where some might be.

As he hovered over the massive man, Brick's size once again shocked him. Maxwell never felt like a giant around anyone, but he normally felt like he matched up, even when his partners were taller than him. There simply was no comparison between Brick and himself, and seeing the giant spread out on the bed, waiting for Maxwell to do whatever would make himself happy was an exhilarating feeling.

Maxwell opened his fingers, and pulled Brick's monster cock against his own. The warm, smooth skin pressed against his was almost too much, both for his grip and for his mind to process.

"Brick, I love your cock."

"Mmhmm," Brick moaned, his eyes closed.

"You're just going to lay there and let me finish myself, right? No matter how sensitive things get, right?"

Maxwell slid his hands up their shafts to give Brick a taste of what was to come.

"Jesus Christ. Are you trying to kill me?"

"Shh. You told me to do what I wanted, right? You'll survive. I promise." As much fun as it would be to torment Brick for a while, Maxwell knew from experience that, while Brick *would* survive, it would switch from feeling good to excruciating in just a few minutes. "Stay still or this will take longer, okay?"

Brick's eyes were wide open, and he'd pulled his hands out from behind his head. Maxwell would have ordered them back in place, except Brick was mostly behaving well enough that Maxwell wasn't going to slow down his own fun over it. Brick's hands were balled into fists to help himself endure the borderline over-the-top feelings of Maxwell grinding their dicks together while masturbating them both.

Brick started panting and growling in rhythm with Maxwell's hand. It was everything. But he didn't flinch. His face was so serious, it was all Maxwell could do to not laugh.

Focus.

Rubbing the dicks together just the way he liked, and already so close to coming from the build-up in the other room, Maxwell knew he'd only need a few minutes. He had no idea whether Brick would make it the whole time, and he wouldn't even complain if Brick pulled away.

Instead, Brick amazed Maxwell by grabbing the sheets even more tightly and continuing to behave as Maxwell's hand moved faster and faster and his grip grew tighter and tighter.

"Oh, baby. This feels so good," Maxwell groaned.

"Good. Come for me, Maxwell. Come for me now," Brick ordered.

It was a clear violation of the role he was supposed to be playing, but it was so Brick and so perfect, that instead of ruining the moment, Maxwell responded to the demanding tone and exploded onto Brick's chest and collapsed onto the bed next to Brick, nuzzling against him as close as he could possibly get.

"Shit, dude," Maxwell gasped.

"I know, right?" Brick agreed.

The two men cleaned up quickly and climbed under the blankets.

As they were falling asleep, and the afterglow started to

fade away, Maxwell tried to convince himself that he wasn't just looking for problems, but as amazing as it had been, it hadn't been quite perfect.

They'd both gotten what they needed, but hadn't done it together.

CHAPTER 12

Brick

"**C**HEESE!" DAVID YELLED WHILE LEANING against the fire truck and smiling for the camera.

"No, no, no!" Maxwell called out, standing up from behind the camera that was mounted on a borrowed tripod.

Brick nearly jumped at the bite in Maxwell's voice.

"What?" David asked, crossing his arms over his bare chest. "Was it my hands? I'm not sure what to do with them."

Brick barely stifled a laugh when David glared at him.

"Not 'cheese,'" Maxwell yelled. "If I hear that goddamn

word again during any of these photoshoots, I'm going to scream."

David, unsure how to respond to the outburst, looked over at Brick again for assistance.

"Maxwell," Brick said quietly, hoping he didn't sound confrontational. "You are *already* screaming about it. What's wrong with cheese? Everyone says it."

Maxwell pointed at David, but kept his eyes locked on Brick. His intensity made Brick feel uncomfortable, and reminded him just how terrifying Maxwell must be in combat situations despite his smaller size. "Say it again."

"But you said—" David started to say.

"Say it again!"

Brick nodded at David, hoping Maxwell would calm down before Brick would have to try and drag him outside to cool off, and wondering if he even could subdue the wild, wiry man.

"Cheese," David said with less enthusiasm.

Brick squinted at the weird face David was making, wondering if he was trying to make some kind of point that would piss off Maxwell further.

"See?" Maxwell shook his finger at David. "'Cheese' makes everyone grimace and look like some kind of stressed-out skeleton." Maxwell snapped a picture anyway. "People are going to love that one, huh?"

Brick tried setting his hands comfortingly on Maxwell's

shoulders, but they were shrugged off immediately. "Maxwell, *you* are what's stressing him out."

Maxwell stepped toward Brick. "No. It's that goddamn word. Say it. Go ahead. It stretches your face into that stupid not-quite-a-smile face that millions of unfortunate kids have been practically abused into making for years."

In a whisper, Brick said, "Cheese," and felt his face stretch strangely. He tried to imagine what he must look like and realized it certainly wouldn't look natural.

How have I never noticed that before?

"Fine. I see your point. So how do we fix it?" Brick asked in as monotone of a voice as he could manage. In the distance, David watched his reflection in the mirror of the fire truck as he said the word over and over.

Brick wondered where the fun man from the previous night had gone. After their amazing romp, Brick had let himself dream of something more. But Maxwell's bizarre behavior in the light of day was making him wonder if they could survive even two hot weeks of passion. Especially if Maxwell was going to be so erratic half the time.

"David. Get in position and repeat after me."

David hurried into position and dutifully repeated Maxwell's words. "Four score and seven years ago..." His eyes darted to Brick for help, but he didn't dare disobey.

When Maxwell gave an order, people seemed to obey.

Images flashed through Brick's head of him following

Maxwell's order to stay still while he had stroked both their dicks in his strong hand. He felt himself getting excited at the thought and had to adjust himself.

David continued. "My father walked naked on this continent, and impregnated my mama." David laughed as he finished the ridiculous sentence.

Maxwell immediately snapped a picture.

Brick looked down at the display. David looked loose and natural, like he was having fun. "Damn, that's...how does that...?"

Maxwell shrugged. "There are several things that are better than cheese-smiles. Having people make funny faces works. Taking their picture when they don't know works. Catching them when they say words that end with 'uh' instead of 'ee' is good too." Turning his attention to David, he said, "That was great. I told you the camera was going to love you. Let's try some with you holding the hose."

David's eyes went wide. "Won't that look a little...gay?"

"Yes. Completely. Is that a problem?"

Maxwell snapped another picture when David laughed again. "No. Not at all. You're the best photographer ever, man."

Maxwell snorted. "Thanks, but don't go putting up billboards singing my praises until you see the finished photos. I'm still learning Photoshop."

David beat his chest and pretended to be angry. "Are you saying I'm so ugly that I need Photoshop?"

"Of course not. You're cover material. But I don't have the best lighting or camera, so I'm going to use the software to smooth out some shadows and shit like that. But I'm not exactly great at it yet. It takes me longer than it should."

Flexing his arm, David asked, "Can you make my arms look a little bigger? I haven't been getting to the gym enough recently."

"Sure thing. I'll make that tiny dick look bigger, too."

Brick laughed when David quickly lowered his hands to cover his crotch.

Maxwell snapped another picture.

After watching Maxwell recover when David started having fun, Brick chalked up his blowup to perhaps too strong of a love of photography. At least everything had settled down quickly this time. And even better, Maxwell didn't need to escape the situation to be able to move on.

Maxwell had been able to shrug it off and come back to his adorable, engaging self. He was certainly fitting in just fine with the guys at the station. Brick knew he shouldn't be surprised since guys were guys when they were locked in close quarters together, and Maxwell was around guys all the time in the Army.

Maxwell confidently pushed David through a few more poses and then started to do the same with Levi. He always seemed to know exactly what each man should do to highlight the best parts of his body. By the end of the session, all the other firemen stood around watching, barely saying a word in fear that they would break the magic.

Brick found the entire thing very sexy, but very cool, too. The more time they spent together, the more Brick wanted from his new friend. He wasn't planning to jeopardize their agreed-upon terms, but that wasn't any reason they couldn't do fun things in between their moments in bed, either.

He whispered in Maxwell's ear while passing behind him between shots, "I want to take you somewhere after this. Just a quick stop before I drop you off and go back out for my last shift."

Brick wasn't looking forward to the shift at all, but there was no way out of it.

It was probably for the best, though. Maxwell hadn't complained at all when he learned Brick had to go to work. He'd just told Brick that he better not cancel any of his vacation days, but he'd be fine lounging alone on the couch after the long photoshoot.

Maxwell certainly did seem to have trouble when he had to do *too much* socializing. Brick bet he'd feel the same way if he had to spend so much time around Maxwell's friends, though. It was hard being the outsider that everyone was judging.

Maxwell had removed the camera from the tripod and was holding it up to his face while walking around to find better angles. Without lowering the camera, he responded Brick's offer. "Okay."

For such a simple word, it had a strong effect on Brick. Maxwell, tired and wanting to be alone, had without hesitation decided that doing something with Brick trumped his own desire to escape to solitude as quickly as possible.

That's gotta mean something, right?

After another thirty minutes of barking orders and the entire fire station jumping to fulfill them, but no further blowups on Maxwell's part, he lowered his camera for the final time. "Great. I think we've got plenty of great shots here. Levi and David, thanks. You guys were amazing. I hope I can do them justice."

David looked up from the chair he'd been sitting in while watching Levi's session and asked, "Do you think I can get copies of the ones I'm in? Quinn loves that sort of thing."

"Sure. I'll fix up any redeye and other basic shit like that and copy them onto a thumb drive. Brick can get them to you somehow."

David's face lit up with a smile. "Maybe we can have you guys over for a meal some night while you're still here, Maxwell. I'm sure Quinn would love to pick your brain for tips for taking better photos."

Knowing that Maxwell wasn't really looking to make friends while he was in town, and having decided that was fine for their relationship, Brick braced himself for an abrupt refusal from Maxwell.

Instead, Maxwell smiled and said, "Sure. If we can find

the time, that sounds fun. The real vacation starts tomorrow, though, so we'll see how many things Brick has planned already."

Brick heard two things.

A reminder that Maxwell would be gone all too soon.

And a sign that Maxwell was interested in growing closer to some of Brick's friends.

Brick decided to ignore the first one.

CHAPTER 13

Maxwell

AXWELL PRACTICALLY BOUNCED AS THEY headed to Brick's car. The photoshoot had turned out to be the most fun he could remember—well, ignoring fooling around with Brick—for a very long time.

In addition to the fun of positioning the men and trying to make them look as great as they could for the calendar, working with Brick had been amazing. After Maxwell's rocky start, Brick had been the perfect assistant. Whenever Maxwell needed something, Brick seemed to already have it in his hand. Whenever Maxwell was starting to tighten up at being watched by all the other men, Brick had the right words to make him laugh and settle his nerves.

He was even better in person than in the emails.

As much as Maxwell thought he'd be able to do a decent job on the calendar, he didn't have much experience actually photographing people in staged settings like he'd been doing all night. Back on base, when he did take pictures of people, he mostly took candids where they didn't even know he'd aimed the camera at them.

Over the years, Maxwell sometimes wondered what he'd do when he retired from the Army, but he still didn't have a plan. It was the main reason he'd never thought of leaving each time it came time to reenlist again. When other soldiers pressed him to imagine life after the military, he would always default to wanting to be a photographer, despite having no idea how to get started.

As they headed down the road, he started to think he could really make it work, and even wondered if right there along the Fox River might be a good place to give it a go...someday.

"So where are you taking me?" Maxwell asked, giving Brick's sleeve a tug.

"There's a shop down on the river that sells antiques and other unique things. I think they're still open. I thought it would be fun to find a few things that I could buy and you could set them up for a photoshoot of sorts since you're going out to do that later anyway. Kind of a thank you for helping us out with the calendar."

The words took away Maxwell's breath. He'd had people buy him gifts before, but they'd always felt a little too close to payments for sex for Maxwell to ever really enjoy them.

Brick held the door for Maxwell. As he walked into the large shop packed full of assorted odds and ends, he was unable to focus on any one thing. He stopped just inside the entryway, trying to get his bearings. "Wow. This is huge."

He felt Brick's breath on his neck when he stepped up behind him and leaned down low to whisper, "I'll never get tired of hearing you say that."

Without giving himself time to overthink the decision, he spun and pressed his lips against Brick's. Instead of flinching away from the public affection, Brick pulled Maxwell against his body and hungrily returned the kiss until Maxwell forgot where he was. With Brick's body blocking his view, they really could have been anywhere.

Maxwell imagined them on a cloud right after a light rain. The sun danced across the raindrops making them shimmer like diamonds. A rainbow arched overhead as the cloud slowly spun in the warm sun.

He smiled as he felt Brick's hand slide down his back and firmly cup his butt. Maxwell started to rub his own hand across Brick's firm chest and let it inch down toward his big...

Someone cleared his throat behind him. "Sorry to interrupt, but, welcome to my shop. Can I help you gentlemen?"

Maxwell tried to break free, but Brick wouldn't let him go until they'd finished their kiss.

"Mmm," Brick hummed before turning his attention to the shop owner. Maxwell blushed, and leaned shyly against Brick's body.

What the hell is wrong with me? I don't get flustered like this.

"I'm looking to buy something for my boyfriend," Brick said.

Boyfriend?

The owner smiled, and patted Maxwell on the arm. "Lucky you." Then he asked Brick, "What exactly are you looking for?"

"Maxwell is a great photographer. He's visiting and doesn't really know anyone, but he's going to be all alone tomorrow while I go to work, so I was hoping to find him a couple things that he could stage and take pictures of to pass the time before my vacation finally starts."

The owner, wearing a tweed jacket that made him look like he should be carrying a pipe, waved his hand in a large circle, encompassing the entire place. "If he can't find something here, sir, then your friend just doesn't want to be taking the pictures." Then to Maxwell, he added, "Can you narrow your interests a bit?"

Maxwell pulled away from Brick, and frowned at an aisle

full of fake flowers. "My boyfriend"—*two can play at that game*—"brought me here without a whole lot of warning. Hmm. Let's see."

Maxwell didn't want to be rude but everything looked too old fashioned. The old schoolhouse-style desk was neat, but it wasn't versatile enough for taking a bunch of photos in one day.

"What I need is something odd and unexpected. Something that I can stage all over town as a weird thing that helps capture the essence of the town...I guess. I'm a little out of my element," Maxwell admitted.

He was much more used to sneaking along the edges of crowds at events while snapping pictures. Even the shoot at the firehouse had been strange because of all the prep work and staging. But now that he was considering it, the thought of staging some interesting pictures instead of just capturing them, was exciting him.

"How about a stuffed animal?" Maxwell finally asked. "I've seen people do that thing where they take pictures of like a little stuffed dog wherever they go on vacation."

"Oh, you could make a calendar out of it like the one you're doing for us firefighters," Brick suggested.

Maxwell found it adorable that Brick sounded more excited about it even he did.

"Maybe. We'll see how the first one turns out."

The owner raised his eyebrows and pretended to fan

himself with his hand. "You'll have to let me know where I can get a copy of that." He turned and waved over his shoulder for them to follow. "This way, please. Stuffed animals are over in the toy section in the back."

The owner walked them straight to a big bin in the back, overflowing with stuffed animals. All three dug in, started pulling out their favorites, and set them aside for a final decision.

When they were done, Maxwell ran his hand over his head. "None of these seem quite right. I think I need something bigger and crazier. I need to be able to take pictures from a distance and still have it show up vividly."

Brick wandered around the corner, leaving Maxwell alone with the owner.

Hugging one of the teddy bears against his chest, the older man said, "Sorry. I don't think I have any bigger stuffed animals around here today. If you leave me your number, I can give you a call if something comes in."

"No worries. I'm sure I'll get some great shots of the river and the trees anyway. But I'll be leaving town in a couple weeks, so I guess I'll just have to be fine without a prop."

The owner nodded, but didn't look happy at not having what a customer was looking for.

"Dude!" Brick called from the other side of the shelves. "This is awesome. There's no price tag. I need to know how much it is."

When he came bouncing back to them, he was carrying a giant green blow-up doll.

"What the hell is that?" Maxwell asked.

"Gumby, man. Don't you dare tell me you don't know who Gumby is or I'll make you watch him all day tomorrow."

Maxwell shook his head, but his focus was on the doll. It was large, taller than himself, in fact. The color was so fake it would stand out almost anywhere. It was odd enough that it could make any scene funny.

Based on Brick's excitement, though, Maxwell wondered if it was a collectable. He didn't want Brick spending a bunch of money on it. "How much is it?"

"Don't you worry your scruffy little face," Brick said, rubbing his hand across Maxwell's stubble.

Yikes. I need to shave tonight. I don't want to give him beard burn.

"Tell you what," the shop owner said with a very serious I'm-doing-business expression that made Maxwell nervous. "You promise to give me one of those calendars when it's done, and I'll let you have Gumby for free."

"Deal," Brick immediately agreed, and offered his hand to seal the deal. "As soon as they show up at the station, I'll bring one down myself. I'll even sign my month."

"Oh." The man rubbed his hand through his long, disheveled, gray-tinged black hair to tame it a bit. "You're in the calendar? You should have said so. I might have tossed something else in for you."

Brick laughed while giving the man a big hug. "Thank you, sir. You're the best."

On their way back to the front door, Maxwell saw a black cowboy hat. He picked it and set it on Brick's head. "We'll need this, too. You'll look great in that hat, no shirt, and a tight pair of jeans. How much?"

The shop owner pointed his finger seriously at Maxwell. "If that calendar isn't here soon, I'll hunt you down wherever you are. Now, shoo, shoo. Get out of here before you steal everything I own."

Brick hooked his thumbs in his belt buckle and walked tall and proud to the car.

Yes. He'll look very nice wearing just that hat.

Maxwell wondered if he'd really be able to talk Brick into letting him take the nude photos they'd talked about earlier.

CHAPTER 14

Brick

I HATE MY JOB.

He knew he was lying to himself, but when he was holding on to the fire engine while it raced to a fire instead of heading to bed with Maxwell, Brick *did* hate his job.

He'd finally found an amazing man to spend a few nights with, and wasn't doing nearly enough of just that. He blew out a breath of air in frustration.

This is the last shift while Maxwell is here, and this fire will make the time pass quickly, at least.

Realizing that his focus was entirely on the wrong thing,

he forced himself to add, *"I hope it's a small, quick fire and no one gets hurt."*

The fire engine pulled up at a house in Brick's own neighborhood. He couldn't remember ever responding to one so close to his home. The idea of a fire so close to where he slept was unsettling. Even though he knew fires could start anywhere, being so close made him think about his own safety. When he confronted fires, he was always able to put on his gear and go in prepared alongside his other firefighters. The poor people he had to pull out never got that advantage.

How terrifying must that be to try and figure out what to do all alone?

With no more time to get lost in his thoughts, he jumped to action, securing one end of the hose to the connector on the truck while Levi hurried off to scout out the fire, which appeared to be more in the back yard than in the actual house.

When he returned, he called out, "It's the shed in back. Burning fast and hot. Smells like gasoline."

Encouraged by the news that it was a relatively small fire, Brick relaxed a bit as he grabbed the end of the hose and followed Levi toward the backyard. Fires from improperly stored gasoline in sheds or garages were not exactly uncommon.

The bright red flames flickered against the left side of the shed. Smoke rose freely above the burning structure. It only took Brick a second to realize that the fire and smoke were not exactly where they belonged.

The smoke should be flowing out from the inside of the shed. Same with the fire. This fire started on the outside and is trying to get in.

It didn't change Brick's job, though.

Bracing himself against the strength of the hose, he opened the throttle. It only took a few minutes to smother the flames.

As soon as he turned off the hose, Levi said what Brick hadn't let himself officially say. "Someone set that fire."

Brick nodded his agreement. "Come on. Help me get this put away."

The word spread quickly through the team, though. Arsonists were on the same level of evilness as terrorists in their minds. Anyone that intentionally set fire to buildings and put other people's lives at risk needed to be locked up for a very long time.

While the shed had been a small, easy-to-contain fire, all it would have taken was a little wind to spread it further in the older neighborhood where all the houses were close together.

"Gangs? Insurance claim?" Levi asked as they worked together to store the hose.

"No idea. Seems like an odd location for that, but who knows? I can't understand why David wants to switch to investigating that shit. It's gotta be frustrating as hell to have most of the evidence burn up before they even arrive. Someone's gotta do it, I guess. I'll just try to take comfort in knowing it's a small fire."

"Yeah, it's a little spooky when they are so close to home, huh?"

Brick nodded as he slapped the safety on the fire hose storage, growing angrier as he thought about how close Maxwell had been to the danger.

Knowing that in the line of duty Maxwell had faced moments way more perilous than the little shed fire didn't make Brick any happier. He liked the guy. Like, really liked him and would do almost anything to protect him.

"You okay, man?" Levi asked. "Don't let it get to you. The odds of it happening at your place aren't any higher than they were an hour ago."

"I'll push it aside. I'm not going to end up going crazy every time someone lights a birthday candle."

"Good. Shake it off and enjoy your vacation."

Everyone rode in silence back to the station, some lost in their own thoughts, all of them fighting off yawns as the sun started to set.

Once they had cleaned and stored all of their gear, Marcus called Brick aside. "Why don't you go ahead and call it a night and go spend a few extra vacation hours with that new guy of yours. We've got plenty of bodies around here, and you've already put out one fire, right? We'll let someone else get any others, if they happen to pop up."

"That would be awesome," Brick said, already backing toward the lockers. "I'll take you up on it and get out of here before you change your mind. See you in a couple weeks."

Brick didn't even bother to shower before heading home. If things worked out right, he'd shower with Maxwell after they got themselves a little dirtier.

CHAPTER 15

Maxwell

MAXWELL STARTED MISSING BRICK HORRIBLY as soon as he'd gone in for his last shift during Maxwell's vacation.

At least he'll be all mine after this one.

Maxwell wasn't even sure how long a shift lasted, exactly. He'd done a Google search that had made it sound like it was probably going to be twenty-four hours. Instead of thinking about how long that sounded, he focused on the beautiful sunset and thinking up ideas for how to use Gumby the next day.

Maxwell meandered the riverwalk looking for spots where

the setting sun created interesting shadows or trails of light. He'd just finished taking a picture of a beam of light sneaking through branches and illuminating a sign reminding people to pick up after their dogs when Nicole called out his name.

She trotted the last few steps to close the distance and punched Maxwell on the arm. "I wondered if I'd ever see you again. Sorry about the other night. Hope I didn't ruin things too badly."

Hoping to hide the memories of how he and Brick had made up afterward, Maxwell looked away. "No. Things are fine now. You just surprised us. How have you been?"

Nicole dragged her foot across the ground and started slowly walking down the path. "Fine enough. Fighting with the boyfriend, but that's not anything new."

Maxwell walked beside her, matching her lazy pace. He couldn't tell whether she wanted to talk about it or not, but he decided to offer her an opening in case she did. "Anything I can do to help?"

Nicole kicked a pebble. "Take me with you when you go?"

"In a heartbeat, if I could." Maxwell was surprised at how quickly he'd gotten attached to Nicole. She was like the sister he'd never had. He had a step-sister out there somewhere that he'd never met, but that didn't count.

Refusing to let thinking about his dad ruin his day, Maxwell turned his attention back to Nicole. "Why don't you just dump him?" He'd asked before but hadn't really gotten a satisfying answer.

"Inertia." When Maxwell didn't reply immediately, she continued. "We've been together a while now. Since high school. Like seven years now. It's just hard to change direction. Plowing forward is easier. Like earlier today, he pushed to move in with me. I don't want that because what's left after that? Marriage?"

Maxwell stayed silent, giving her space to organize her thoughts and say more. Instead she shook her body, as if trying to get something unpleasant off her. "How many more days are you in town and where is your firedude?"

"Ten. And working."

"What the hell? You came all the way here to visit, and he couldn't even take time off to do something with you other than the sexy bedtime stuff?"

Maxwell laughed at her outrage on his behalf. "Nah. It's not like that. He didn't have enough vacation days for my whole trip. He's actually on his last shift at work right now. He'll be all mine starting..." he glanced at his watch, "actually, I don't know exactly. Whenever it ends."

"Excellent. Do you have any big date plans? Chicago? Great America? Baseball game?"

While it was fun to see Nicole's energy level change as she talked about his relationship rather than her own, it did remind him that they really didn't have plans other than fooling around in bed. After that trip to the antique store, it really felt like they *should* have some events planned.

"What do you recommend?"

"Me? I think you should just fuck for two weeks. I mean, it's not like you're planning on coming back around, right?"

The words were a slap to Maxwell. Despite that being exactly the plan, he didn't like other people reminding him so bluntly. Especially with some of the private thoughts he'd been having about Brick.

"I don't really know." The words fell out slowly. "That *was* the plan. It's not the first time I've met people just for a single vacation, I'll admit."

Nicole bumped her shoulder against his. "You dirty dog. So what's the difference this time? Is it me? Say it's me."

Maxwell spun, grabbed Nicole and dipped her. "Of course it's you, my dear. It's always been you."

The two giggled as he pulled her back up.

"I'm not sure," Maxwell continued. "Or I'm pretending I'm not sure because it's easier than admitting that I like the guy. The actual guy, not just his body, which is amazing, too."

"I'll say. So what's the plan, Stan?"

Maxwell raised his camera toward Nicole. "I'll take pictures when I have free time. I'll do whatever Brick is willing to do when he's available. And I'll let my heart get crushed when I leave, I guess." Maxwell pointed to a patch of light just off to the side of the path. "Go stand over there so I can take your picture."

Nicole hopped eagerly to where he pointed. "What kind of pose should I make?" She held her hands around her face like Madonna's Vogue.

"Not that. Umm. Look up to the sky like you are seeing heaven open up for you?" She was beautiful and innocent as she looked skyward. "Perfect. You look like an angel that landed here in this little patch of Earth next to me."

"Gag me, man. Does Brick fall for that stuff?"

Maxwell took her picture.

"I don't know what Brick falls for." They both started walking along the path again. "We're still trying to get to know each other. Oh. You're not going to believe this. He bought me this giant, green, inflatable Gumby thing to take around town and take pictures of. I'm going to do it tomorrow while he catches up on sleep. It should be hysterical."

"Aww. He bought you a present that sounds like a sex doll. How sweet!"

"Okay. Thanks for making it creepy. Let's go back to the douchebag you're with. I think you should dump him immediately. I'll have Brick set you up with one of his coworkers and we'll double date."

"Damn, that sounds tempting. But the douchebag would still be around and he's jealous as hell. I wouldn't want him doing something stupid and ruining your time here. Who knows what that big dummy would do?"

Maxwell pointed to a nearby footbridge that crossed the river. Nicole hurried over and flashed him a smoldering look with her pouty lips pursed together. He snapped the picture. "Okay. It's official. You have to come out with me and Gumby tomorrow morning before Brick gets home. We'll do a Beauty and the Beast thing."

Nicole waved away the compliment. "Fine. I'm off work anyway and it'll be better than sitting around waiting to argue with Billy."

"I can't believe your big, tough guy has a name like Billy. Based on what you've said and what he did when I met him, he seems like a twerp that enjoys bullying people to remind himself that he isn't as pathetic as he thinks he is."

"Don't ever say that around him. I made a joke about his name one time and..." her words trailed off, but her hand rose to her cheek.

Maxwell's head spun to survey the area as if Billy were going to pop out of nowhere and try to hit Nicole again. "Nicole, dump his ass. If he's hit you before, he'll do it again. Cut this off. I'm here to protect you."

Nicole turned and walked back the way they'd come.

"Nicole, where are you going? You're just going to let him abuse you? I swear to God I've got your back."

He meant it, too. He'd do anything to keep Billy away. If she just gave him the word, he'd walk straight to where Billy was and beat the shit out of his cocky, smug face.

Nicole stopped long enough to turn, stomp her foot, and nearly shot at him. "You've got my back? For how long? Ten days until you leave me here all alone, right?"

She turned and stormed off again.

Maxwell followed after her, feeling sick to his stomach when he realized what he'd suggested. "Whoa. I'm sorry. I'm being an ass. I can't just barge into town and start demanding that you change everything. I just can't stand the thought of some dude hurting you." Seeing the pained expression on her face, Maxwell thought that what she needed more than anything was a friend, not some cop questioning her and treating her like she'd done something to deserve whatever Billy had done. "But I'll behave and do whatever you want so we can stay friends while I'm here."

Nicole didn't slow down, but after wiping tears from her eyes, she reached down and squeezed Maxwell's hand. "Thanks. I know you're right, but I don't have the courage to do it, and that makes me mad. I want to move away, but don't have the courage to do that either. I feel very trapped and just want a friend."

Maxwell pulled her close and wrapped his arm over her shoulder. "I will happily apply for the position."

"Okay. I'll get back to you in a couple weeks when I go through the rest of the applications," she joked.

The two talked about locations they should take Gumby to in the morning while they walked back toward the houses.

As they approached Nicole's, a neighbor ran up, shouting, "Oh thank God you're okay."

"What are you talking about, Mrs. Duncan?" Nicole asked, leaning even more tightly against Maxwell.

"There was a fire." When Nicole started sprinting toward her house, the woman quickly added, "It was just to your shed." When Nicole stopped and turned back questioningly, she added, "But I was still worried because I'm a worry wart. The house is fine. Sorry to scare you."

Maxwell followed Nicole into her backyard. The ground near the shed was muddy and the one side of the shed was mostly destroyed. But the lady had been right, there was no other damage.

"What the fuck?" Nicole asked, looking at Maxwell with large, nervous eyes.

He shrugged. Brick would know what to say, but all Maxwell could offer was, "Maybe the gas for the mower?"

"Shit," Nicole said, looking back at the shed. "I guess. Fuck, at least it didn't explode and blow up anything. Oh my God. What if it had and someone was nearby? I could have killed someone."

Her body started shaking.

Maxwell rushed to embrace her and drag her back toward the house. "Hey," he whispered in her ear. "You didn't do anything wrong and no one got hurt. It was just an accident and everything is going to be fine."

He kept talking in what he hoped was a soothing voice while walking away from the scene. It had worked for several men he'd fought alongside in the Army.

It seemed to work for her, too. By the time they reached her door, she grabbed her keys without being prompted.

"You want me to come in and stay with you for a while?" Maxwell offered.

"No thanks. Go home and get ready for your fireman. I'm going to take a bubble bath and read in bed until I fall asleep. I'm not really in the mood to talk," she said, stepping into her house.

"Okay. Call me if you change your mind. I'll come over or just hang with you on the phone. Whatever you want."

Nicole gave him a quick hug. "Thanks. I still want to play with you and Gumby tomorrow. I'll be fine by then, I'm sure. Take care."

"You too."

The door closed before Maxwell could try and talk her into letting him stay around longer.

While walking back to Brick's place, he couldn't help but wonder how a fire could start inside the shed, burn the outside of the shed, but not seem to really burn through the wall.

He couldn't shake the suspicion that someone had caused that fire. As much as he tried to convince himself that he was missing something obvious, he knew in his heart exactly who had started it.

Billy.

Maxwell practically shook from frustration knowing that he couldn't prove a damn thing. To make matters worse, if he accused Billy he'd probably lose Nicole as a friend and might even get her hurt.

Fucking Billy.

CHAPTER 16

Brick

EXHAUSTED, BUT HAPPY TO BE starting vacation a little early, Brick burst through the front door, bounded down the hall, and scooped Maxwell up off the floor so he could cover him with kisses. Maxwell wiggled and pushed away, before giving a grunt and meeting him kiss for kiss with an almost angry energy.

When Maxwell nipped his tongue with his teeth, Brick nearly pulled away to ask what was wrong. But Maxwell wrapped his legs around Brick's hips and ground his hard-on against Brick's stomach.

Fuck it. We'll talk later.

Maxwell sucked against a vein in Brick's neck. Brick knew it would leave a hickey, but it felt so fucking amazing that he couldn't have stopped the attack if his life depended on it.

"I've got to get out of these pants," Brick said. "My dick is trapped and if I get any harder, it'll snap in two."

With his lips still pressed against Brick's neck, Maxwell purred. "You smell like shit. Let's take a shower."

The vibrations from Maxwell's words tickled his nerves that were already heightened and responding to every move Maxwell made. "There was a—"

"I don't give a shit. I just want your dick in my hand and for you to not smell so bad."

Brick laughed while carrying Maxwell toward the shower. "Fine. Since it's your nose that's offended, I'll let you be in control of the soap."

"You're talking too much."

Brick was more than happy to shut up. He had his own needs pounding through his body.

Once in the bathroom, Maxwell hopped off Brick and turned on the shower. Brick was in the middle of pulling his shirt over his head when Maxwell pulled him in under the water while both men were still completely dressed.

The water hadn't had a chance to warm yet. Brick flinched against the cold blast against his back and tried to turn away from it.

"Don't move. You need to protect me, Mr. Fireman. Don't let the mean, cold water get me."

Brick grimaced, but didn't move. The water was cold, but if Maxwell wanted to be in charge again, the water was bearable enough as long as it warmed up soon.

"I won't let the mean, cold water touch you, Maxwell."

He tried to lean forward to encourage another kiss, but Maxwell gently pushed him away. Before he could ask what Maxwell wanted, he grabbed the collar of Brick's soaking shirt that was clinging to his body and tore it wide open.

The aggressive move reached a primal spot in Brick's soul. He wanted to howl. He needed to get them both naked.

Instead, he forced himself to stay still and wait for Maxwell to give his next order. The water warmed, allowing Brick to relax his muscles, which made the waiting a little easier.

Maxwell worked on Brick's pants, but the water made them hard to pull down.

As he continued to struggle, he said, "Shit. We should have undressed before getting in."

"I tried to—"

Brick cut his words short when Maxwell managed to pull his pants down enough that he could squeeze his testicles a little more firmly than was comfortable. "What was that, dear?"

Rather than risking saying the wrong thing, Brick shook

his head and breathed a sigh of relief when Maxwell's fingers loosened and started massaging instead.

As much as Brick was starting to unwind and enjoy the moment, Maxwell's eyes were still wide and angry about something.

What could have happened while I was gone? I wish he'd talk to me.

Maxwell gave up trying to tug Brick's pants down. Instead he unzipped his own and was able to spring his dick free. Brick reached out to grab the beautiful, wet cock, but Maxwell slapped his hand away.

He squirted soap into his palms. Grabbing a dick with each hand, Maxwell squeezed tightly and started vigorously jacking them both off.

"Fuck. That's...Fuck." Brick gave up trying to sound sexy.

The soap provided plenty of lubrication, but Maxwell's grip was so tight that it bordered on uncomfortable while still feeling absolutely fantastic.

He knows what I want better than I do.

Steam filled the shower as Maxwell continued working both dicks. Brick knew he wouldn't last much longer, but didn't bother to warn Maxwell and risk getting his balls squeezed again. If Maxwell wanted a quickie handjob, Brick certainly wasn't going to argue. They'd have plenty of time for more throughout the rest of the evening.

Brick noticed that Maxwell seemed close, and was taking

no steps to slow things down. The man clearly knew what he was doing. Through the steam, Brick could barely see further than Maxwell, but what was the point in seeing anything else in the heat of the moment?

He's perfect. And he's mine.

He ignored the voice that added, "For two weeks."

With his eyes wide open, he watched Maxwell. His eyes had glossed over, staring at some unseen thing between them as he focused on working both of their cocks, slowing one hand when one of them seemed closer to finishing than the other.

Eventually, his eyes met Brick's, and he smiled. The smile undid Brick, unleashing his orgasm right as Maxwell also came, shooting his load against Brick as Brick returned the favor.

"I have no idea how you do that," Brick said. "I completely lose it when I'm under your control."

Maxwell laughed and rubbed his hand across Brick's chest, and leaned in for a kiss.

"I'm glad you liked it. Now hand me the soap so we can get fresh and clean."

They both wrestled out of their clothes while the hot water pounded against their bodies.

While Maxwell lathered the soap on the washrag and started washing Brick's chest, Brick finally dared to ask, "You doing okay? You seemed on edge earlier. Did something happen?"

Maxwell nodded.

When Maxwell didn't say anything, Brick added, "Do you want to talk about it?"

"No. Not really." Maxwell traced a finger through the running water rolling down Brick's chest. It felt like he was struggling between not wanting to say any more, and not wanting to offend Brick. He appeared to struggle with his next words. "There's nothing I can do about it. Don't worry. It doesn't have anything to do with you. Here, do my back."

Brick took the washrag that Maxwell offered and started rubbing his back when Maxwell turned away.

"What are you doing home early, anyway?" Maxwell asked.

Brick let him change the subject. "We had a small fire earlier and when we got back, the boss told me to cut out early and enjoy my vacation. So far, this is the best vacation ever."

Maxwell leaned back against Brick's body. He felt so warm and comfortable. Brick draped his arms over Maxwell's body and rubbed his chest.

"Glad to hear it," Maxwell said. "Hey, you can come with me and my friend, Nicole, to take pictures of Gumby tomorrow, if you want."

"I didn't know you had plans *with* someone," Brick said, hoping he didn't sound annoyed.

"Well, you were supposed to be working or sleeping or whatever. I had the whole Gumby day planned, remember? I suppose I could cancel, but Nicole really is so sweet and I think she could use some nice people in her life. In fact, it would be great if you and her buddied up for..." Maxwell's body went tense.

"No, it's fine." *I guess.* "Will you have time for a real date with just the two of us tomorrow, though? I want to get dressed up and go to a nice place. Show off my hot, new boyfriend, you know?"

Maxwell didn't hesitate. "Absolutely. I wouldn't have scheduled this thing with Nicole if I knew you were coming home early, but she had a really shitty day."

"Hey, man, it's really okay. Seriously. I dragged you out with my friends and will do it again while you're here, I bete. I'm looking forward to meeting your friend for real this time. I was just a little bummed that the first moments we'll spend together on my vacation will be with me as the third wheel."

"What are you talking about? Your vacation started already, right? This was how you started the vacation." Maxwell flicked Brick's dick with his finger to remind him and then reached behind Brick to turn off the water. "What do you say we head to your room and do our second thing of your vacation before you get too tired and fall asleep on me?"

They dried each other off, sneaking kisses onto each other's body. Brick was surprised that he really couldn't wait to spend time with Maxwell and Nicole in the morning. It would be one of those moments that felt more like a relationship than just a fling.

Brick was pretty sure that when Maxwell was gone, those were the things he would remember about his visit.

CHAPTER 17

Maxwell

W HEN BRICK EFFORTLESSLY LIFTED THE park bench, his muscles flexing against the thin fabric of his t-shirt, Maxwell was just barely able to not gawk too obviously. He noticed that Nicole wasn't as successful, or just didn't give a damn. With her mouth hanging open and her hand grabbing ahold of Maxwell's arm as if for balance, she watched Brick carry the park bench to where Maxwell indicated.

"Does he have a straight friend?" Nicole whispered to Maxwell. Before Maxwell could reply, she turned her attention back to Brick. "Maybe it would look better if he moved the bench over there," Nicole said, pointing a few feet to the left while nibbling her lip.

Brick shrugged and leaned over to grab the bench.

Maxwell rolled his eyes and playfully shoved Nicole away. "No. Right there is perfect, Brick."

Nicole stomped her foot, but carried Gumby to the bench. The breeze had picked up and Gumby was having trouble staying in his seat.

"Why don't you sit down next to him and hold him in place? Brick, you go around behind and look like you're mad because Gumby moved in on your woman."

They had been taking silly pictures for a couple of hours. Any thought of Brick being disappointed had faded long ago. He seemed to be having the most fun of any of them.

"I should have brought the cowboy hat," Brick said as he moved into position.

"If you had, I wouldn't be able to keep my hands off of you," Maxwell said, while trying to find the right angle for the shot.

"Sure. Rub it in," Brick answered, waiting patiently.

Maxwell thought something was missing but couldn't figure out what, until he saw the flower shop next door.

"No one move. I'll be right back."

Maxwell bought one rose and handed it to Nicole when he returned. "Okay. Smell the rose and pretend that Gumby gave it to you while Brick was off checking a baseball score."

"That bastard," Brick yelled, shaking his fist.

"Oh, yes. Do that."

Nicole held the flower to her nose. Brick held his fist out toward Gumby. Gumby seemed to smirk in the sunshine.

Maxwell exhaled and snapped the picture between breaths, just like he did when he shot his gun. He took a few more shots as backups even though he knew the first had been perfect.

"Okay. That's a wrap. Let's get some lunch. I don't know anything around here. Where should we go?"

"The taco place across the river," Nicole said first.

"Deal," Brick immediately agreed while rubbing his stomach.

Maxwell made a mental note to go out of his way to treat Brick's friends as amazingly as Brick was treating Nicole.

I definitely need to be as good to his friends as he's being to mine. No more crazy mood swings allowed.

Maxwell wanted to ask if she'd heard from Billy again. If things worked out, they might be able to talk her into leaving him and going on a date with one of Brick's friends. But he worried that talking about her boyfriend would upset her and ruin the good time they were having, so he left the topic alone.

The last thing he wanted was to have another perfectly fine moment with Brick ruined.

"Hey, Nicki. What the fuck are you doing with these dicks?" Nicole's boyfriend said from behind Maxwell.

Fuck.

Just hearing his voice made Maxwell's fists clench. He wanted to punch the idiot in spots that would quickly draw blood and bring concussions. Instead, he stayed put and ground his teeth.

Brick, however, moved to step between Nicole and Billy. Maxwell wanted to kiss his brave hero. He barely knew the girl but was still willing to protect her from assholes like Billy.

Nicole rose and stepped in front of Brick, leaving Brick scowling ominously behind her. "We were just screwing around taking some pictures. I thought you were working?"

"They fired me." Billy shrugged as if asking if she could believe their nerve. "Claimed I stole some shit."

Maxwell didn't like the way Billy's hands rested on his hips. He looked a little too ready for violence. Maxwell wasn't worried about whether he and Brick could subdue him. Maxwell could do it alone, and would have bet a lot of money that Brick could, too. But guys like Billy would start a fight, accept the beating, and collect money in a lawsuit. Plus, Billy would be able to use the beating as leverage for getting Nicole to feel sympathetic toward him.

"Did you?" Nicole asked icily.

"Yeah. But they can't prove shit. The assholes are profiling. Whatever. I'll collect unemployment. It'll be like a paid vacation. Come on. Let's go get lunch. You're paying, though, since I lost my job."

Maxwell spoke before he could remind himself to stay out

of her business. "She's already got lunch plans. She's coming with us. I'm paying to thank her for helping me out with these photos." He made sure to not even hint that Billy might be invited, too.

Billy turned his attention fully onto Maxwell. Maxwell didn't back down, but didn't do anything to look aggressive either. He knew he'd be able to move fast enough if Billy did something stupid.

"No one asked you, asshole," Billy said with a how-stupid-is-this-guy laugh. "Why don't you and your boyfriend get back to the privacy of your own house where you belong before you give some of the kids around here some bad ideas?"

"Wow," Brick said, blinking in shock at the homophobic outburst.

He was opening his mouth to say more when Maxwell shook his head to beg him to stop. In the moment, nothing mattered to Maxwell more than making sure that neither he nor Brick did anything to make Nicole's life any worse. Maxwell was pretty sure that if they embarrassed him out in public, he'd take it out on her when they were alone.

Brick looked angry, but fortunately didn't say anything.

After quickly apologizing for needing to miss lunch, but completely ignoring Billy's rude behavior, Nicole stomped away with Billy close in tow. Billy watched them over his shoulder the entire way, looking like a wild dog hoping that the humans would provoke him in anyway.

How does a nice girl like Nicole end up with a creepy fuck like Billy?

When they turned and disappeared around the corner, Brick finally broke his silence. "What the fuck? You're just going to let her go away with him?"

"Don't, man. I feel like shit about it, but what am I supposed to do? If she wants help, I'll be the first to knock his ass to the ground, but we've already talked. She doesn't want me to do anything. As frustrating as it is, I can't just beat the shit out of him because it would make me feel good."

"He's going to—"

"I hope not, but until I see him do anything real, what choice do I have? I want to kill him...literally. But I'll be the one that ends up in trouble if I do. Until Nicole is willing to take a stand, or I catch Billy doing something..." he couldn't even let himself think about what kinds of horrible things Billy might do. "I don't know what I *can* do."

Brick closed his eyes, seemingly as frustrated as Maxwell. "All you can do is be her friend and hopefully help her see that she deserves more." He sounded pissed as he agreed with Maxwell.

The two faced each other silently, their bodies tense with energy that needed to be released. Maxwell was about to suggest finding somewhere with a heavy punching bag that they could swing away at, but Brick spoke first.

Brick forced a smile. "She's been with him a while, right?

There must be something that she likes about the guy. Maybe we don't know everything."

Maxwell sighed. It was convenient to think that all the world's problems were overseas in the countries the Army sent him to. Convenient, but not realistic.

"Yeah. I know. I'll be okay. We were just having such a good day, you know?"

Brick stepped directly in front of Maxwell and rubbed his shoulders. "Hey, do you still want to go out to eat? If not, that's fine. We can just go home, but if you're up to it, my offer to take you out to lunch still stands."

It wouldn't be the same as pounding all of his frustrations against a punching bag, but it was definitely better than doing nothing. Besides, Maxwell didn't want to let Billy ruin his day any further than he already had.

"Sounds great. Let's go home and clean up, though. I'm sweaty. Besides, I brought a nice dress shirt that I should put to good use some time during this trip."

"Yummy," Brick said as they turned to walk back to his house. As they crossed the first street, Brick grabbed Maxwell's hand. "There's something special about you, Maxwell Cope. I'm glad we stumbled across each other on the pen pal exchange."

"Me, too," Maxwell readily agreed. "As much fun as those emails have been, being here with you is so much better."

CHAPTER 18

Brick

M AXWELL LOOKED AMAZING IN HIS white button-up shirt and gray dress slacks. He'd left an extra button at the top of his shirt undone and Brick couldn't stop stealing glances at the visible parts of a tattoo on his exposed skin. It was such a small patch of skin, but in some ways, seeing it in the middle of the restaurant was sexier than seeing him naked at home.

It's because he left that button undone just to tease me.

They'd changed their minds on the Mexican food and gone to a Chinese restaurant right on the river instead. Out on the balcony, their table overlooked the river. The shade from the building's overhang combined with the ceiling fans and a gentle breeze made the temperature perfect.

Rather than ordering separate meals, they'd ordered a few dishes and agreed to share them all. While they waited for the food to arrive, they sipped their iced teas and chatted.

"How long have you lived around here?" Maxwell asked.

"Forever. I had some time away in college, but I've lived pretty much inside a ten-mile circle the rest of my life." Brick ripped open two sugar packets and poured the sugar into his tea.

"You ever think of leaving?"

Brick wondered where all of the personal questions were coming from. They seemed a little out of character.

Has something changed?

Trying not to get his hopes up, he said. "Not too often, but sometimes the urge hits me really strong for a couple weeks. But where would I go, right? Everyone I know and care about is nearby. Moving would mean losing all of that. I'd need a pretty compelling reason to give that all up."

He silenced the voice in his head that said that Maxwell was pretty compelling.

He lives overseas in places I can't go even if I wanted to.

"Yeah, I don't blame you. If I had all that, I wouldn't want to leave it behind either."

Before Brick had a chance to turn the question back on Maxwell and maybe learn something about him, the waiter arrived with their food. Brick set his napkin on his lap while the food was set in front of them.

"Damn, that smells great." Maxwell scooped some white rice onto his plate.

"It does," Brick agreed. "I've heard of how good this place is, but never made it here before. It just opened recently. It used to be an Irish pub."

Maxwell glanced around at the restaurant, with its bamboo plants, and walls stuffed full of pictures of dragons. "That's impossible to imagine."

"Yeah, they had some really corny leprechaun shit. There was a wall painted green with a rainbow that ended in a pot. They had this game. Whoever could throw a foam ball in from some ridiculous distance won the pot of gold, which was just a free meal. I almost got it one time, but someone opened the front door at the wrong time and a gust of wind blew it off course at the last second."

Maxwell wasn't wasting any time loading the rest of his plate.

"We never get any good Chinese food on base. The meat's always too gristly and there's too much MSG or something."

"Dig in, soldier. We'll order more if we run out."

Brick's stomach grumbled, demanding that he get started on his own plate.

They ate in a comfortable silence until their plates were

empty. Brick scooped up more food, and picked up his chopsticks.

"I've never figured out how these work," Brick said. "But it's fun to screw around with them."

"Chopsticks? Really? It's like this."

Maxwell grabbed his own pair, set them easily in his hand, and started shoveling food into his mouth just as easily as he'd done with the fork.

Brick tried to imitate Maxwell's easy movements, but all of the food he picked up fell back to the plate before reaching his mouth. Brick was used to feeling like a lumbering clod, though. Delicate things were not his strong suit at all. He shrugged and set the chopsticks on the edge of the plate. "I'll just use my fork."

"Here, like this." Maxwell slid over to the seat next to Brick, and grabbed Brick's hand.

Brick would have preferred just sitting next to each other holding hands like that and talking some more, but Maxwell was on a mission to teach him how to use his chopsticks. He placed Brick's hand around the chopstick and adjusted the sticks until he nodded in satisfaction.

"Good. That's most of the battle right there. Now you do this with your fingers."

Feeling Maxwell's rough fingers moving against his own was distracting. He couldn't focus on what he was actually supposed to be doing.

"No, not like that. Like this." Maxwell leaned in closer and tried to make Brick's fingers work the right way.

Being so close to Maxwell's body was too much for Brick. *To hell with eating!* He leaned forward and pressed his lips against Maxwell's neck. While sucking lightly, he inhaled his boyfriend's faint, musky scent.

"You smell like such a man," he said with a growl against Maxwell's skin.

Maxwell cleared his throat, but didn't pull away. "Is that good?" he whispered.

"Fuck yeah, it is. I've been looking for a man like you for a very long time."

Shit. That's too much.

Maxwell did pull away that time, but not in a hurry. He stared into Brick's eyes, and patted his cheek.

"Careful what you say or I might fall for you."

Brick couldn't believe he'd heard Maxwell correctly. It matched what he was feeling, no matter how many times he'd told himself to keep his distance to protect himself for when things would need to end. Letting his guard down, he asked, "Would that be such a bad thing?"

Maxwell smiled, but his eyes were sad. "Probably." He seemed to want to say more, but couldn't find the words.

Brick felt their relationship hanging on a precipice. It would take even less than the gust of wind that had blown his foam ball off course to completely change the direction of their relationship.

"This is going to sound stupid, but I want to be with you, Maxwell. And not just for two weeks. I know the odds of us making it through the long times apart are slim, but they are zero if we don't try, right?"

Maxwell slid back over to the seat across from Brick. The move tore Brick's heart from his chest.

Now, that was definitely too much. I've even ruined the two weeks we could have had because I got greedy.

Maxwell blinked at Brick a few times without saying anything. Brick was almost ready to flag down the waiter for a check when Maxwell finally nodded and said, "Okay. I think it's a horrible idea because we're both going to get hurt so badly, but I'm going to be hurt even worse if we don't try. So what the hell."

Brick felt like there should be fireworks exploding above them to commemorate the moment, but instead had to settle for the grin that spread across Maxwell's face that was more dazzling than any firework Brick had ever seen.

Feeling happier than he could remember feeling in years, Brick stabbed a piece of shrimp with the end of his chopstick, shoved the food into his mouth and waggled his eyebrows at Maxwell.

"Are you trying to impress me with your caveman ways?"

Maxwell asked, delicately nibbling a water chestnut slice as if to show Brick just how wild he was behaving.

Brick pointed his chopsticks at Maxwell. "You're lucky I'm not using my hands to shovel the food into my mouth as quickly as possible, and then tossing you onto my shoulder to carry you back to my bed."

"Lucky? I mean, sure, that first part sounds gross, but the whole on your shoulder back to your bed...I think I could live with that."

Brick turned and made eye contact with the waiter. "Check, please."

While the waiter hurried off, Maxwell said, "We're completely missing something important."

Fuck. I knew it was too good to be true.

Trying to sound calm and casual, Brick leaned back on his chair tipping the front legs a few inches off the ground. "Oh yeah?" While his mind scrambled to figure out what he was missing, he said, "Well, I'm sure we can take care of whatever it is."

Maxwell stood and stretched his arms high over his head, exposing his stomach and the faint trail of hair that crept down into his pants. Brick wanted to shove his hand down there and feel that cock. Rather than worrying about the complexities of long-distance relationships or even the simpler two-week fling, Brick just wanted some good dick. That would take care of everything.

"Damn it, I can't think when you look sexy like that. What am I missing?"

Maxwell stepped between Brick's legs and sat on his thigh. Brick knew everyone in the restaurant was looking at them.

Fuck 'em.

Still, he blushed at the attention he felt pressing on the back of his neck.

With Maxwell's face inches in front of his own, so close that his eyes merged into one, Brick wanted to kiss him until the restaurant closed or their breath ran out. But he wanted Maxwell to think he could be a mature lover instead of just a lust-filled caveman.

"Please, man," Brick begged. "You're killing me. What am I missing? Whatever it is, I'll give it to you. The moon? It's yours."

Maxwell laughed. "Brick, you're perfect. It's nothing like that. This is a big moment for us, right? You and me? Giving this a shot? It seems like that should be marked by something more than shrimp and sweet and sour pork, you know?"

Is he looking for a gift? It doesn't feel like that's what he's saying at all, but if not that, then what? Brick's entire body was on fire knowing that they were so close to reaching something Brick had never experienced before. He wasn't ready to call it love, but he wanted to.

It could be. We just need the time to justify the way I'm feeling now.

"Tell me, please."

Maxwell cocked his head slightly. "A special moment like this needs a kiss. Like in the movies. Something we'll remember forever."

Without waiting for Maxwell to explain any further, Brick attacked his mouth and kissed him with every ounce of lust and love and fear and hesitation that had been trapped in his body. Maxwell didn't back down from the aggressive, passionate kiss. He met him ounce for ounce, seeming to unleash demons of his own.

Brick had no idea what the fuck was happening. It was too big for him to comprehend or even keep track of, but he knew that he would forever remember the moment, if not the details.

There were now two parts of his life. Everything that had happened before the kiss. And everything that was to come.

All the hurt and longing and loneliness of the past were still there, but they didn't matter anymore. They'd just prepared him for this one perfect moment with Maxwell and should be celebrated for their role.

Maxwell's hands explored Brick's chest, face, arms, hair, neck...they never seemed to stop. Brick, on the other hand, had his grasp securely on Maxwell's hips. He wasn't ever going to let him go.

"I'll just leave this here. You can pay whenever you want." The waiter whispered, but it was enough to bring them back to reality.

Clearing his throat, Brick said, "Thanks."

Brick tossed more than enough money on the table to cover the bill and a tip while Maxwell whispered the dirty things he wanted Brick to do to him when they got home.

"Can we go home now or are we forgetting something?" Brick asked.

Maxwell asked, "Do you have condoms?" Brick nodded. "Lube?" Brick nodded again. "Then all I need is you."

Brick didn't lift Maxwell onto his shoulder, but he did guide him through the restaurant and to his car with a firm nudge in the back. He had big plans for as soon as they got home.

CHAPTER 19

Maxwell

WHAT AM I GETTING MYSELF into?

Standing on the precipice of having actual intercourse with Brick was one thing. That didn't even really faze him all that much. But preparing to have sex while at the same time starting to have real feelings for him was a whole different ball of wax.

He'd never let himself have feelings for the men and women that he'd vacationed with in the past. It had always been completely effortless for him to focus on the fling and the fancy houses, protect his heart, and enjoy the fun times.

Somehow Brick had pushed through that barrier and

Maxwell didn't know what to do about it. He knew he should fake a headache or phone call. Hell, even pretending to get called back to duty for an emergency mission would be better than letting himself continue to grow closer to Brick.

Instead, he found himself hard as a rock, with his underwear getting wet and sticky, and saying things like, "Drive faster, Brick."

Brick kept his eyes on the road, but smiled at Maxwell's encouragement. "I'm trying. There's just too many people walking around downtown. Don't these people have jobs?"

Maxwell rubbed Brick's thigh and managed to slide his hand up to Brick's swollen cock before getting it slapped away.

Brick groaned and banged his hand in frustration on the steering wheel as two moms pushing strollers passed in the crosswalk ahead of them.

Finally, the last person cleared out of the way and the light turned green. The car lurched across the intersection, turned onto a small side road that had much less pedestrian traffic, and a couple of minutes later, they were running up the stairs inside Brick's house.

It only took a few seconds more for them both to get naked and dive into bed.

Maxwell closed his eyes, giving himself the opportunity to find any reason to back out. Without understanding why, he knew that if he forged ahead, things would change between them. Everything in the restaurant had just been words.

Making love after that conversation would cross a line he wouldn't be able to uncross with Brick.

Not that I want to. Right?

Instead of letting his uncertainty discourage him, though, Maxwell tried embracing his earlier bravado and let himself follow wherever the moment was leading.

If Maxwell thought he had a chance of turning down a relationship with Brick, it disappeared the second Brick's warm lips wrapped around his dick. The slurping sounds coming from Brick's mouth were primal and raw. They were the prelude to fucking, plain and simple.

And Maxwell needed that.

Brick made eye contact for a split second when he pulled his lips away, spat on Maxwell's dick, and lunged back in place to continue the blowjob.

Damn, damn, damn.

Everything was perfect. Maxwell's only complaint was that he didn't have a complaint.

If we take this step, there's no backing down. Things either work out or I get crushed when they don't.

He refused to acknowledge that he already knew it wouldn't work out.

"Brick. Hold on," Maxwell begged. "You're going to make me come too fast. Let me catch my breath."

Brick kind of obeyed. He pulled Maxwell's dick out of his mouth. Instead of letting him actually catch his breath, though, Brick pushed Maxwell back so he was propped up on the pillows, and then straddled Maxwell's chest and shoved himself into Maxwell's mouth.

Unlike the first time, Maxwell was ready for Brick's unrelenting face fucking. He grabbed the meaty cock and felt the heft of it as it slid through his hands and lips.

He's like a fucking jackhammer.

After just a few seconds, Brick shocked Maxwell by pulling away, running to his dresser with his dick bouncing.

"Where are you going?" Maxwell asked, wondering if Brick had gotten hurt or remembered that he had somewhere more important to be.

"Condoms. Lube." He stopped digging through the top drawer and looked back at Maxwell, almost guiltily. "That is if it's okay. Are you really ready for that?"

A thousand voices screamed in Maxwell's head that this was his last chance and that he should take it to protect himself. They were the same voices that kept him from making any permanent attachments with anyone in the past. Other than the guys he fought beside, Maxwell hadn't let himself really get attached to anyone in years.

And, truth be told, he was lonely. He wanted someone like Brick that he could have some continuity with. Someone who could give him a reason to return to the same place for a second visit, and maybe send him care packages with cookies in them while he was deployed.

I deserve it, too. I'm a good guy. I'm not my dad.

Holding a condom in one hand and the lube in the other, Brick waved them both at Maxwell and raised his eyes questioningly.

But am I really any better than him? He left me and Mom without a second thought, and I do the same to people all the time. Maxwell didn't know. But he wanted to be better. He wanted to finally fall in love.

"Hell, yeah, I'm ready," Maxwell replied, still overwhelmed with how quickly everything was happening. "Fuck me, you sexy fireman."

"I don't know if I'm going to be able to hold back. You better hold onto something before I knock you off the bed."

Staring at Brick's giant dick as he walked back toward the bed, Maxwell's mouth practically watered even as he wondered at his size. Brick tore the condom wrapper with such ferocity that the condom jumped out and landed on the bed.

Maxwell, unsure if he was trying to convince himself or Brick about how onboard he was with everything, picked up the condom. "Let me help with that."

Brick flinched when Maxwell set the cool condom against the tip of his warm skin. When Maxwell tried to unroll it onto Brick's dick, it wouldn't work.

"Hey, I think you have it the wrong way," Brick said with a gentle laugh.

Maxwell's ears warmed as they turned red. "Fuck. I've never tried putting one on someone else."

"A first. Let's celebrate it, man." Brick held his hand up with his palm facing out.

After a second pondering what he was supposed to do, Maxwell laughed and high-fived the hand. "You're such a dork," he said with a laugh.

When Maxwell flipped the condom over, it worked easily, stretching to contain the beast. Maxwell hoped he'd have as easy a time when Brick shoved that cock inside of him.

"Lube me up. Go crazy with it, okay? Feel free to use the entire goddamn tube. Should I go on my back or doggy-style?" Maxwell asked.

"Whichever you're more comfortable with, but I'd like to be able to see your face either way."

Since it would be easier to keep eye contact while taking a good pounding if he was on his back, Maxwell rolled back onto the bed and set his legs up in the air against Brick's chest, while listening to the hammering of his heartbeat. "Okay. I'm ready."

Spreading a large amount of lube on his fingers, Brick smiled dangerously at Maxwell.

Oh my God. He wants this as badly as I do.

Maxwell's toes curled in anticipation, reminding him that he was going to really need to focus on relaxing all of his muscles or it would never work.

Without asking if he was ready, Brick pressed his hand between Maxwell's legs. Maxwell ignored the coldness, instead focusing on the sensation of Brick's fingers playing across his ass. The little tingles as Brick circled the rim of his entrance forced a delighted moan from his lips.

"That feel good?" Brick asked absently while he focused on the work at hand.

"So good, babe."

Hoping to encourage Brick to slide a finger inside, Maxwell shimmied his hips.

"What's it like?" Brick asked, continuing to slowly circle without even increasing the pressure.

Maxwell's dick twitched anxiously. He needed more. "It's hard to explain. It's like...well, if I'm being honest, it kind of feels like you're afraid to stick your finger in my ass. What's up with that?" He wiggled his hips again.

"Sorry, it's just hard to do anything but stare at your amazing body, man."

"Brick, we have a saying in the Army. I'm not sure where it's really from, but, 'The only way out is in.' I'm butchering it a bit, but if you don't press that finger into me, I'll show you how the Army deals with traitors."

Brick laughed. "As tempting as that sounds, I'll take a rain check."

Maxwell's encouragement worked, though. There was a moment when he didn't think he was going to be able to shake off the last of his lingering doubts about embarking on their relationship and relax enough for anything to happen, but then he let out one last breath, focusing on how incredible Brick was in every way. An instant later, Brick's middle finger was exploring inside of him.

"Dude, you're so tight." Brick said in a near whisper.

"I've been saving myself for you," he said, trying keep his face serious.

Brick rolled his eyes. "Yeah, right. Hold on."

Maxwell lay back and focused on really feeling Brick's finger, which was curving toward his belly and curling as if beckoning Maxwell to him. It all felt really great, but Maxwell wanted more.

He was just about to tell Brick to use his dick instead of his finger when it hit something that plucked every nerve in his body for a second like Brick was some fucking guitar rockstar before moving on just a little to the left where it had almost no effect.

Still panting heavily from that one magical moment, and gripping the sheets in his hands, Maxwell asked, "What was that? Do it again?"

Brick smiled. "Did I find it?"

Then the finger was back. Maxwell spread his legs wider, and placed his hands on his stomach as if trying to hold Brick's hand in place.

Not that Brick needed any encouragement. He stroked

that sensitive little bundle of nerves over and over, making Maxwell feel like he needed to pee, and come, and scream Brick's name forever.

Maxwell had read about how great it felt to have the prostate rubbed, but no one had ever taken the time to find his before.

"Brick...whoa, whoa. Hold on. I want you in me when I come."

Watching Brick lick his lips at the suggestion was almost enough to push Maxwell over the top. When Brick didn't move, Maxwell grabbed Brick's wrist and pushed his finger out. He immediately felt empty and craved to be filled again in a way that he'd never known he needed until Brick opened a new world for him.

He needed Brick's dick.

"Come on, Brick. Give me what I need."

Brick added more lube, both to the condom and to Maxwell. With his hand wrapped around his cock, Brick pushed the tip where Maxwell needed it.

That cock is so big.

Making himself breathe slowly and stay calm, Maxwell set himself to relaxing his muscles again, not believing for one second that it was going to work out. He nearly cried in frustration.

Brick whispered, "I've heard that if you kind of push out, it makes it easier."

Maxwell knew it. *This isn't my first rodeo.* Trying to push out without tensing muscles was no easy trick when staring at Brick's thick cock.

He was as ready as he'd ever be, but Brick was being too gentle. "Brick, it's great that you're trying to take it so easy on me, but I think you're going to need to push a little bit or this isn't going to work."

That was all the encouragement Brick needed. After a small grunt, Brick slowly but steadily pushed his way in. Maxwell made a mental note to send a thank you letter to the company that made the lube that allowed this impossible and insanely incredible moment to happen.

Brick didn't need any further prodding. He slowly started sliding back just far enough that Maxwell worried that Brick would pull out, leaving him empty again, before he insistently inched his way back in. His dick was so long that there was no hope of Maxwell taking it all, but Brick was somehow able to tell exactly how far he should go.

Maxwell wanted to say something to mark the occasion, but as Brick increased the pace, every time he tried, he could only grunt. Realizing that he wasn't doing anything besides laying there, Maxwell reached up and pinched Brick's nipple, earning him a stronger thrust.

"Do it again," Brick said.

Instead, Maxwell wrapped his hand around Brick's neck and pulled himself up so he could suck on his nipple. He almost let go when he realized that he wasn't touching the bed anymore, but Brick had no trouble holding him in the air while continuing to fuck his ass.

How can he be so fucking strong?

The shift in angle changed something and suddenly Brick's dick was attacking with shallow, quick strokes that magic button that his finger had teased earlier.

Maxwell whimpered at the shocking pleasure that coursed throughout his body. He had no idea why, but a tear rolled down his cheek. "Don't stop," he begged before biting down on Brick's skin.

Without slowing one bit, Brick said, "You're killing me, man. My nips are so sensitive."

"Fuck you. You think that's bad. You're hitting my goddamn prostate like it's a fucking punching bag, man. Your poor little nips are nothing compared to what's happening in there."

Brick's laugh was quickly replaced with a look of concern. "That feels good, right?"

"If by good you mean that it feels like I'm about to lose my mind, start drooling, and agree to anything you want just so you'll keep doing it, then, yeah, it feels okay. I need to come, man. So badly."

"Shit. It sounds like I'm on the wrong end of this," Brick said, rubbing his hand against Maxwell's cheek.

Maxwell leaned toward the hand and sighed in joy.

"Totally. Next time, I'll get you, but right now, I just need to come. Please, Brick."

With a serious expression on his face, Brick nodded. "Me, too."

While still standing, Brick somehow slid his hand between their bodies and started stroking Maxwell's dick while continuing to fuck his ass. "Will this work? Are you close? Because I am. Come for me, Maxwell."

Maxwell once again obeyed, coming between their bodies while Brick fucked him even harder and faster, sending fresh aftershocks through Maxwell's body until he thought he'd died and gone to heaven.

Surely people don't feel this good on Earth.

When Maxwell seriously worried about blacking out and falling to the floor, Brick finally thrust one last time and screamed Maxwell's name loud enough the neighbors had to have heard before tossing Maxwell back on the bed, tossing the condom across the room, and collapsing next to Maxwell.

"What the fuck are you doing to me?" Brick asked. "You're amazing."

Maxwell glowed at the praise. "Whatever you want me to do, Brick. Whatever you want."

The words sounded strange coming from his mouth, but only because for once, he actually meant them.

Both men tried to talk for a few seconds just to show how

much they cared for the other, but neither lasted long before drifting off to sleep with a smile on each of their faces.

CHAPTER 20

Brick

BRICK LEANED AGAINST THE KITCHEN counter, tapping his toes as if that would help the toast finish faster. Maxwell was at the kitchen table, skimming the newspaper comics.

"Do you follow football at all?" Brick asked.

Maxwell nodded and sipped his coffee. He seemed lost in his own little world in the light of the new day. Brick hoped he wasn't having second thoughts.

Needing to talk after what had happened last night, but not sure what to say, Brick continued. "I keep up with baseball during the season, but don't watch that much unless I'm doing it with friends. I listen to it on the radio while working out when I'm alone. Football is my passion, though. Especially college. I'm a big Illini fan."

"Yeah. I follow Nebraska," Maxwell replied absentmindedly.

"What? I thought only people from Nebraska liked them Huskers."

Still without looking up, Maxwell said, "Yeah. That's where I'm from. Lincoln."

The toast popped up, cutting off any replies from Brick. While he carefully pulled the toast from the toaster, just barely managing to avoid burning his fingers, he tried to remember an earlier conversation. "I thought you said Montana or Idaho or something like that."

Maxwell turned a page and shook his head. "Not me. Nebraska born and raised. You must have me confused with one of your other boyfriends."

Frowning, Brick set the toast on the table and headed to the refrigerator for orange juice.

I guess I could be wrong. It's not like we've known each other long enough that I know everything about him.

"Must have," Brick agreed, deciding that, no matter what, it definitely wasn't worth arguing over. "Hey, what exactly do you do in the Army?"

Maxwell finally lowered the paper and looked up at Brick. "I try not to think about it too much when I'm on vacation.

I'm sure you're the same, right? Who wants to deal with all the crazy stuff you must see during work when you are trying to relax?"

Brick knew firefighters like that, but he wasn't one of them. Talking about the hard moments often seemed to help him process and move past them.

"Sorry," Brick said, buttering his toast. He hesitated long enough to open the jar of jelly and spoon some out onto the bread. "I just want to know more about the real you rather than just the vacation you, you know?"

Maxwell nodded. "I do. Sorry, it shouldn't be hard for me to talk about any of it. I'm just being weird. Like I'm worried about saying something that will ruin what's happening with us. What if I tell you something real and you decide that it's just too much?"

With his mouth full of the first bite of his toast, Brick grunted. Once he'd finished swallowing, he asked, "But can we have something real if we're afraid to talk about things?"

Grabbing his own toast and taking a bite after dunking it in his coffee, Maxwell said, "I do a few things, but the most dangerous one is when we do patrols. I'm the point man. We walk through villages and cities that have been flagged as harboring bad guys. Terrorists, mostly."

Maxwell set the rest of the toast down. His hands made a dive for the newspaper, but he seemed to will himself to set it down and make eye contact with Brick. "When we get the clearance, we go door-to-door at the houses the powers that be tell us to search. Sometimes we get let in nicely and are guided through the house to see who or what is inside."

His eyes fled Brick's face and looked out the window. His body looked ready to follow and leave Brick behind for good.

Brick wanted to say anything to comfort him. He wished he'd never brought it up, or that Maxwell had stayed in the comfortable realm of talking about watching movies and playing ping-pong on base.

We're not ready for things to be this real.

After a deep breath, Maxwell, still staring out the window, barely blinking, continued. "Sometimes we don't."

Brick wanted to just nod and change the subject. Instead, in a whisper, he asked, "What happens then?"

Maxwell's sad smile broke Brick's heart. He wanted to rush to him and wrap him in a hug.

Before he could move, Maxwell said, "Then I break down the door. Guns at the ready, we storm through the house. We scream loudly in Pashtu or whatever language it seems like they might speak. We tell them that they need to get the fuck on the ground, and that if they just follow orders, no one will get hurt." Maxwell's voice got louder just telling Brick about it.

Brick couldn't even imagine that kind of life. He'd broken down plenty of doors in his days and screamed loudly after doing so, but never in a hostile way.

He lives in a completely different world.

Maxwell's hands tightened around his coffee mug. His mouth opened, but no words came out.

"If you don't want—" Brick started to say before Maxwell interrupted him.

"Most of the time, it works out just fine. Our heart rates spike, and time slows down, and we're sure we're going to die, but most of the time, everyone in the house just drops to the floor, we search the house, and go on our way. You'd be surprised at how few real terrorists there are in the world considering how much fucking trouble they cause."

Brick nibbled on his dry lips, trying to imagine what it would be like to storm through a house while hoping to not get ambushed by hostile people with guns, the whole time knowing that the other people in the house hated you for being there in the first place.

"Damn. That sounds so hard. I mean, I could deal with the adrenaline and chaos. We deal with that whenever we have to go into a burning house. But we're always trying to save everyone inside, and when we're done, we get cheered for our effort. No one is ever trying to kill us. Fuck, I don't know how you do that. Does it even feel worthwhile?"

Maxwell ignored the question. "One time, we marched into this house. Everyone was screaming and yelling at us. I think it was some kind of wedding or birthday party. There must have been a million friends and relatives all over the place. They were pissed, but they hit the ground and shut up quick enough. The place was eerily silent after all the yelling. I turned a corner and saw a gun. The bastard shot and hit my leg. It hurt like hell. I shot back before I had time to realize what the fuck was going on." He paused and sipped his coffee. "He dropped to the ground screaming. Only then did I realize I'd shot some kid with a paintball gun."

Brick had carried dead people from burning buildings, he had watched them die before the paramedics could save them, and he'd heard of some dying after they reached the hospital, but never had Brick even been close to the reason they had been hurt in the first place.

"Did he die?"

"No. Fortunately, I clipped his arm. But that's just bad luck. If I'd been doing my job right, he would have."

Brick had no idea what he was supposed to say. "How did you get through that?"

"Went back to the practice range to improve my aim. Sorry. Gallows humor. We get by it by focusing on the mission. There are some really bad guys out there and it's our job to find them and either capture or kill them. That job, like yours, can help keep many innocent people alive. I just try to remember that when we go through the fucked-up shit and mistakes get made."

"Fuck." It was all Brick could think to say.

"Yep."

Needing something to do, Brick grabbed both their coffee cups and headed to the counter to refill them.

"Well?" Maxwell asked.

"Well, what?" Brick replied, hoping that Maxwell was trying to change the subject.

"Well, is that the deal breaker? Are you done with me because my life is too fucking crazy? Who wants to date the guy that will probably get shot or blown up or captured and tortured to death? Or even worse, come back home full of PTSD and not fit for living with."

Brick hadn't even gotten around to thinking that far yet, but knew the answer right away. "I'll be here for you. Whatever happens, we'll work through it, right? It's not like my life is squeaky clean. I can get killed in the line of duty, too. I can get shaken from things that I see or that happen to me or the other firefighters. Are you willing to take that same risk with me?"

"Touché. Hmm. I guess I am. After all, you know where I'm from. It's not like I can escape, right?"

Brick shook his head. "No way. You try to run, I'll track you down. Even if I have to trek through Afghanistan or wherever you're at to find you. I better start my paperwork for a passport."

Brick smiled when Maxwell laughed at his corny joke.

Maxwell hoped they could move back into safer territory. "I don't think you'd survive the flight. All those hours cramped up in a seat on a commercial flight."

They laughed at the image of Brick all scrunched up in the middle of a row with screaming kids on each side of him.

Brick carried the coffee cups back to the table. "Oh, fuck it. I'm calling this whole thing off. There's no way I can handle that!"

"Hey. I have a confession. At least, I think I do. Did I tell you I was from two different states?"

Brick nodded.

"Well, I always lie about real stuff with the men and women I hook up with. It's stupid, but, well, I'm kind of stupid sometimes. Nebraska is real, though. That's where I'm from. When we go visit my mom someday, that's where we'll go."

When Brick set Maxwell's mug in front of him, Maxwell grabbed his shirt and pulled him down for a kiss. It was just a quick, simple, peck on the lips. But after their conversation, it felt like so much more.

"This is crazy, right? What are the odds of this working out?" Maxwell asked.

"With two badasses like us, I'd like to see anyone try and break us apart."

Maxwell pretended to karate chop the air. Brick flexed his arms.

"You might have something there," Maxwell said. "Who could be tough enough to hurt us when we team up against them?"

Brick pounded the table. "Fuck yeah. You know what this needs? A celebratory team meeting in my bed."

Maxwell sprang from his chair and raced him down the hallway.

CHAPTER 21

Maxwell

FOR SOME VISUAL VARIETY IN the calendar, Maxwell decided to take the pictures of Clay outside down by the Fox River. Maxwell and Brick arrived early to scout the area and settled on a spot beneath a tall tree alongside the river at a section with a dam and little waterfall.

Clay sweated in the hot sun, but otherwise looked like he was having a blast, while Maxwell ran around snapping pictures and shouting things like, "Hold the ax on your shoulder," and "Make sexy eyes at the camera."

Brick was sitting on a nearby picnic table, watching their every move. Every time Maxwell needed anything, he hopped to action with a smile on his face that threatened to distract Maxwell from his task.

Even the passersby couldn't help but stop and watch, the ladies frequently whistling their appreciation at Clay's muscular body, glistening from the sweat.

Only poor Ezra looked miserable. Maxwell didn't know what to do for him other than get through Clay's pictures as quickly as possible. He would happily have included him in the pictures with Clay, but the other firefighters had insisted that no civilians be included because then their wives and girlfriends would want to be in it too.

So instead, Ezra jumped up between each shot and swiped at Clay's hair and dabbed the sweat from his face while clicking his tongue continuously at the whole affair.

"Ezzie, relax," Clay told his husband when Maxwell twirled his finger to hurry things along. "I'm fine. Can you just go sit down and relax? I'll take you wherever you want to go when we're done."

"You big dummy. I just want to be here with...oh, sorry. I'll go sit down and let Maxie finish."

Maxwell didn't bother correcting the nickname. He'd tried, but Ezra had just looked at him as if he'd been talking in a foreign language. It seemed that if Maxwell did succeed in getting Ezra to change, he'd just wind up with a different, and possibly more embarrassing, nickname.

At least he isn't calling me Max.

Instead, he focused on the pictures. He was pretty sure he already had plenty, but as long as Clay wasn't burnt out, he knew he couldn't have too many.

"Okay, turn your back to me, look over your shoulder and flex those back muscles. Yeah. God, yeah. Like that. And smile." Maxwell took several pictures in rapid fire "Shit, they are going to eat this up."

"Hey, don't get too excited," Brick called out. "Clay's a married man."

Ezra clicked his tongue again. "Maxwell is too rough to be Clay's type. He likes the pretty boys like me." He batted his lashes to prove his point.

Holding the camera to his face still, Maxwell snapped some pictures of Brick and Ezra together at the table. "You don't have anything to worry about from me, Ezra. Who in their right mind would want to date a fireman, right?"

He continued snapping photos while Brick charged at him from the table, tossed him over his shoulder, and tickled his ribs.

"Mercy! Uncle!" Maxwell squealed. "You're lucky I have this camera or I'd kick your ass right in front of your friends."

"Ezra, can you take his camera to make this a fair fight?," Brick said, not setting Maxwell free. "I've heard plenty of his macho bragging, but, personally, I don't think he has the stones."

Saving his energy, Maxwell let his body go calm until Ezra had taken his camera.

As Ezra backed away, taking pictures of the two preparing to fight, Maxwell whispered into Brick's ear, "Stand down now, hon, or I *will* embarrass you in front of your friends."

"We'll see. I've heard about enough of how badass you are. Let's see what you've got. I went to state in wrestling in high school, you know."

Still hoisted up over Brick's shoulder, Maxwell coolly held his thumbs up for the camera. "Whatever, man. I kill people for a living. You probably think that means I need to hide behind a gun, but sometimes guns attract too much attention, so we have to use our hands."

He didn't know why he was sounding so creepy and ominous. Would it really be so bad to throw the match and end up pinned underneath Brick on the warm, soft grass? Rather than backing down, though, Maxwell focused on keeping his breathing calm, preparing for a fight he wasn't going to lose. After all, Brick was the one who had started it. He was the one who deserved to eat a little dirt.

Loudly so Ezra and Clay could hear, Brick called, "Loser walks back to the car in their underwear. Deal?"

Ezra laughed and shouted, "I think Brick just wants a chance to walk around in his undies."

"Sure." Maxwell agreed. "Are you going to put me down or

do I have to start trapped up here?" He'd already begun calculating moves, trying to make sure he didn't actually hurt Brick during the display.

"You saying you need me to put you down to have a chance?"

"No," Maxwell answered bluntly.

"Shit." Brick chuckled. "I'm going to get my ass kicked, aren't I?"

"Yep."

Brick moved quickly without saying another word. He slammed Maxwell toward the ground, spinning him around so he could drop his massive weight on Maxwell's back, hoping to wear him down.

With enough time, it would have worked. Brick had clearly been a decent heavyweight wrestler. But Maxwell had no intentions of giving him that time.

The way Brick was holding him, Maxwell's first move usually would have been to just smash his head into his nose, but he liked Brick's nose. Instead, he lifted his left leg and quickly drove the edge of his shoe down the inside of Brick's leg.

Maxwell escaped when Brick's hands relaxed and his balance shifted from the pain and surprise.

"Damn, that hurt." Brick said hopping on his good leg a couple times before settling and regaining his balance. Maxwell had hoped that once he'd escaped, Brick would call a truce. Instead, Brick said, "It's gonna be like that, huh?"

"When you aren't fighting for wrestling belts, anything is fair game. If we lose out in the real world, we die…if we're lucky."

Brick lunged.

Maxwell easily ducked under, sidestepped, and tripped Brick. As Brick flailed to catch his balance, Maxwell realized that he didn't know how he'd end this without actually hurting Brick.

"Seriously, man, let's just walk away, okay. You're too big and strong for me to really subdue you easily. So I'm either going to end up making you pass out or seriously hurting you."

The look in Brick's eyes said that he'd realized the same. "Want to call a truce?" Brick asked.

Maxwell quickly nodded. "Yeah, let's shake hands and go get a beer."

"Hell, no," Ezra called out.

Maxwell had completely forgotten the other men were still there.

"What?" Brick called over to them, turning his back to Maxwell.

Clay nodded. "I was promised that the loser was going to walk to the car in their tighty whities."

Ezra pointed in their direction. "So someone better start stripping down."

Brick laughed and looked around to see how many other

people were in the area. "Well, at least we're mostly alone, I guess. I'll fall on the sword."

Maxwell, hoping to turn the spectacle into something fun and memorable, whispered. "The way I see it, no one won. So that means we both lost, right?"

Maxwell made no move to resist when Brick spun to face him and gave him a long, slow kiss. Once again, the background faded for Maxwell. He couldn't believe how much Brick's kisses affected him.

Clay eventually coughed to get their attention.

"Good news, Ezzie," Maxwell said. "We've decided that we both lost."

"I don't see how that's good news at all," Ezra said.

Maxwell pulled away from Brick and undid the button on his pants. When he looked over at Brick, he'd already done the same.

"Oh dear," Ezra cried out.

"You guys are really doing this?" Clay asked. "We're going to end up getting arrested." He didn't tell them to stop though. "Hurry up."

Giggling the entire time, both men stripped out of their pants. Maxwell wished he were wearing boxers like Brick instead of his boxer-briefs.

Ezra apparently had a different opinion. "Brick, those boxers are hiding all the good stuff. You need to get some decent underwear like Maxwell's."

Clay and Ezra helped pack up the gear, and they all laughed while running across the field to where the vehicles were parked. After quick hugs, Clay and Ezra jumped into Clay's pickup and sped away.

Maxwell pulled on his pants and climbed into the passenger seat. When Brick joined him, Maxwell asked, "Where to?"

"Somewhere with some serious air conditioning. Movies or a bar?"

Maxwell really didn't care. "Either sounds fine as long as I'm with you."

"Corny, but okay. We'll go to the movies, then. We'll find one no one else is watching and kiss in the dark like we wanted to do the other day."

Maxwell perked up at the thought of making out in the public theater. As corny as it sounded, it was true; anywhere sounded good as long as Brick was there.

CHAPTER 22

Brick

RICK WALKED PROUDLY THROUGH HIS city with his boyfriend by his side, hoping people he knew would pass by and see him.

"This city's amazing." Maxwell said, squeezing Brick's hand. "I haven't lived in a place that was so convenient to walk around in before."

They had decided that it would be silly to drive the mile to the theater when the weather was so nice.

"It's funny," Brick said, taking in the city as if for the first time. "I've lived here forever and tend to drive way more than

I should. Having you around is making me look at this place a little differently."

"We should check in on Nicole on our way back home after the movie. Maybe take her to get some ice cream," Maxwell suggested.

"I won't ever argue about...shit."

Brick pulled his phone out of his back pocket and dialed 9-1-1 as soon as he saw the smoke down the street. When Maxwell asked what was wrong, Brick pointed down the block. It was the same house as the one where the shed had been set on fire the other day.

That's either some really bad luck or there's something fishy going on. We'll have to make sure someone's investigating whatever is happening.

"Oh my God! That's Nicole's house!" Maxwell yelled.

They ran to the house together and joined the crowd outside while the call connected.

"9-1-1, what's your emergency?" a woman dispatcher asked.

"Fire on Mission Street. Shit, I don't know the number." The smoke and fire made it impossible to read the address.

"204 Mission Street? If so, we have an emergency crew on the way. They should be there in a few minutes."

"Great. I'm Brick Swan of the Batavia Fire Department. I'll work on getting the crowd out of the way while they get here."

"Very good, sir. Is there any sign of anyone in the building?"

"I can't see anyone. This is the house that had the recent shed fire, though, so I'd put money on this being intentional. Tell the cops to hurry their asses."

Brick turned toward the tug on his sleeve. Maxwell stared up at him wide-eyed. "It was Billy, wasn't it?"

Brick held up a finger to tell him he was almost done with the call and would hurry to get it finished.

Maxwell's attention had already turned back to the house. "Brick. Nicole's inside."

Squinting to try and see what Maxwell was looking at, but only seeing smoke and flames, Brick told him, "The fire department will be here in a second. If she is inside, they will find her."

"You're the fire department." Maxwell looked panicked.

Brick would need to pay special attention to keeping him calm once he was done with the call. "My boyfriend thinks he sees his friend, Nicole something or other, in the house. About twenty-three or so. She is the owner of the house. She has a boyfriend that I don't think lives there who may also be inside. He probably started the fire. I'm going to put you on speakerphone. My boyfriend is close to hyperventilating, I think. Tell the fire department to hurry."

Maxwell was walking slowly toward the house. Brick hurried to pull him back. "Help me get everyone across the street."

Maxwell didn't look like he'd be particularly useful, but at least he'd stopped inching toward the house.

"Everyone, I'm a firefighter. The engine's on its way. Please back up across the street so we can do our job."

As usual, the crowd followed his orders. People were always looking for someone to take charge during emergencies. Before he could feel proud of his achievement, Brick realized that he'd lost track of Maxwell in the chaos. Worried that Maxwell was throwing up or had passed out at the thought of Nicole in danger, Brick pushed through the crowd, but didn't find him on the ground behind them.

He glanced at his watch and finally understood why people always complained at how long it took for emergency crews to arrive on the scene. Time passed differently while you were waiting.

The cheering from the crowd shook him from his thoughts. He turned to follow the sound and nearly had a heart attack when he saw Maxwell on the front porch of Nicole's house.

What the hell's he doing?

Maxwell flinched when he touched the hot doorknob. Instead of coming back to the safe side of the street, he backed up a few steps before charging the front door and slamming it with his shoulder. Brick had done the same move dozens of times. Based on Maxwell's good form, he had, too.

A thick cloud of smoke exploded out the opening.

He's going to get himself killed.

"Where are they?" Brick screamed into the phone.

"One second." He could hear the dispatcher clicking the keyboard. "It looks like they are at the train tracks. Not moving. So they must be waiting for a train."

"Did you call someone from another station?" Brick demanded.

"Yes, sir. But they won't be there for another ten minutes."

Brick knew that he was supposed to stay on the line and wait for the fire engine to arrive. He had yelled at many idiots who thought they'd be a hero and try charging into burning buildings. He also knew that he would die standing around waiting for the fire engine to arrive while Maxwell was risking his life trying to save his friend.

He tapped an old woman standing nearby. "Hold my phone. I have 9-1-1 on the line. Answer any questions she asks."

Brick didn't bother to repeat himself when she asked what was going on. He pressed the phone into her hand and, before commonsense could convince him otherwise, sprinted across the street to do whatever he could to help Maxwell while promising to kill him if they made it back out safely.

When the smoke inside the house engulfed him, Brick felt naked without his protective gear. Unsure where Maxwell had gone, he froze for a moment at the entryway of the raised ranch house, trying to decide whether he should go up or down the split stairway. He heard a bump at the top of the stairs and saw Maxwell struggling with a kitchen table chair in the middle of the living room.

Hurrying to his side and trying to ignore the smoke and heat, he finally noticed that Nicole was bound to the chair. Her face was covered with tears, sweat, and running mascara. A scarf or rag had been wrapped around her head, covering her mouth. Brick considered removing it, but figured it might be helping keep some of the smoke from her lungs, which reminded him of the danger he and Maxwell were in.

"Help me with these ropes." Despite Maxwell shouting, Brick could barely hear him.

After a quick look at the knots, Brick knew they would be too hard to untie in the horrible conditions.

"That'll take too long. We'll just carry her out the door."

He tipped the chair and grabbed ahold of the back and nodded for Maxwell to grab the feet. Maxwell didn't need any further encouragement. Now that he had a plan he had no trouble following Brick's lead. With two people carrying the chair, they were able to make it down the stairs fairly easily and escape out the front door.

Fresh air had never tasted so good. He wanted to collapse on the ground, but knew they needed to get further from the burning house.

"Hold on, Maxwell. Get across the street before you put her down."

The crowd cheered seeing them carrying a girl, but they quickly made a hole to let them through.

Brick and Maxwell struggled with the knots until an older guy tapped Brick on the shoulder and held out a pocket knife. "Will this help?"

"Thanks." Brick quickly grabbed the knife and started cutting through the strips of fabric around the woman's ankles and arms, quickly freeing her.

He tried handing the knife back to the owner, but shock seemed to have locked the man's arms to his sides. It didn't matter, though. They'd gotten Maxwell's friend out of the house.

And Maxwell was safe. He'd already removed her gag. Nicole still sat in the chair, but she seemed as okay as she could be, having gone through whatever the hell had happened in the house.

When Maxwell stood to walk to Brick, Nicole pulled him down against her, clinging to him like he was a lifeline.

It wasn't far from the truth, Brick realized. Who knew what would have happened to her if Maxwell, with no concern for his own safety, hadn't been crazy enough to run into the burning house?

As Brick fell to the ground in relief, he heard the sirens. A minute later, the fire engine and ambulance arrived on the scene. The paramedics quickly tended to Nicole in their cold, professional way. The crowd was abuzz with gossip and the firefighters were barking orders, but Brick couldn't make out any of it.

He barely noticed when Maxwell followed Nicole into the ambulance.

Instead he watched from afar as his coworkers started prepping to fight the fire.

CHAPTER 23

Maxwell

*H*OURS PASSED IN THE WAITING room of the hospital with no word from Nicole. She'd been hustled away so that the paramedics could check on her lungs and look for any other injuries. When his head drooped again, Maxwell stood up to try and stay awake. After shaking his limbs to keep the blood flowing, he wandered over to the vending machines, put a dollar in the one with the coffee, and selected coffee with cream and sugar. The cup fell into place, but only a few drops of coffee dripped into the cup.

"Dammit!" Maxwell banged his fist against the machine in frustration.

Bouncing on the balls of his feet like a boxer staying loose between rounds, hoping it would get his blood flowing, he moved around the waiting room. He didn't recognize any of the people in the room with him anymore. Everybody that had been there when he arrived had long since left.

"Hey, you," a man called from behind him.

Maxwell turned, quickly and aggressively at the voice, but relaxed with a sigh when he saw it belonged to a nurse holding a steaming mug of coffee out to him. "The machine broke earlier today. The repair guy won't be here till tomorrow. I'm not supposed to do this, but you looked like you could use a drink. Just don't tell anyone where you got the mug if they ask."

Maxwell gratefully accepted the mug. "Thanks. Some whiskey would work too, but this is probably better all things considered. Do you have any news about my friend, Nicole? She's a little younger than me. A little wild and crazy, but she's probably exhausted after whatever you guys are doing to her back there."

The nurse shrugged. "I haven't heard anything about her, but if she's been here as long as you say, I'm sure she'll be wrapping up soon. I just got here, but if I hear anything I'll let you know." The nurse turned and walked away before Maxwell had a chance to thank him for the coffee.

Maxwell blew across the top of the steaming drink to cool it down, and tried to take a sip. There was no cream or sugar, and it was still too hot, but just the smell of the coffee beans was enough to refresh his tired brain.

He'd just sat back in a chair when a door opened and Nicole walked through it, looking exhausted. She'd found time to wash away the tears and makeup, but her hair and clothes were still a mess. She ran straight to Maxwell and wrapped her arms around him.

He returned the hug while asking, "How are you doing? Everything go okay back there?"

She nodded her head that was pressed against his shoulder.

The bastard that did this is still out there.

Changing topics to distract her from her problems, Maxwell said, "Well, you look great. I've certainly looked a lot worse just after boring nights of drinking. I don't know how you stay so pretty."

Without pulling away, Nicole said, "Stop talking. I'm not sure whether to roll my eyes or laugh at you, and I'm too tired to do either. Just hold me."

Maxwell did as she asked.

He looked up when a cop walked up to them and cleared his throat. Despite using Nicole's name, he talked to Maxwell. "Nicole, sorry to bother you. I just have one question for right now. Where are you planning to stay tonight? We want to make sure we have the area on patrol, just in case."

Nicole looked like she was about to cry again at the thought of needing the protection. Taking a deep breath, she managed to stay composed enough to say, "I'm not sure. I don't really have anywhere else to go. A hotel, I guess."

Maxwell shook his head. "No, Nicole. You'll stay with Brick and me, of course and don't even think about arguing. You've been through too much to make a good decision on this, so just say yes, and do whatever paperwork they need you to do so we can get out of here."

She squeezed him tightly, which was all the answer Maxwell needed.

The cop asked them to write down Brick's address and collected both their phone numbers. "Sorry for what you went through tonight, ma'am. If you notice anything odd, please call us immediately and we'll hurry over to help out. Don't worry about false alarms, okay? And sometime tomorrow, we'd like you to come in and answer some questions."

Nicole quickly agreed.

The cop offered to give them a ride home, but they turned him down, wanting to stop on the way home to buy some essentials.

When the cop walked away, Maxwell called for a cab and paid extra for him to wait for them while they hurried through Wal-Mart to buy a toothbrush and pajamas.

Several times as they walked around the store, Nicole apologized for interrupting Maxwell's booty-call vacation.

Maxwell's mind hadn't even gone there yet, but when it

did, he mentally shrugged and said they'd work it out. One nice thing about their new relationship was they had time. It would probably make finding private moments together during this trip more awkward, but there'd always be next time.

San Diego! I need to email him and cancel the trip.

Trying to ease her nerves and make it sound like she wasn't any imposition, Maxwell joked, "I'll just have to remind Brick to be quiet when we sneak off to fool around later tonight. If you turn up the TV loud enough, I'm sure it'll be fine."

Maxwell was a little surprised at how little it bothered him that Nicole moving in would limit the amount of sex that he and Brick could have, but somehow, taking care of Nicole with Brick's help seemed like an even more intimate thing to do. It felt very real and grounded. It definitely wasn't the kind of thing that people did during a fling.

Maxwell couldn't resist throwing a few cans of chicken noodle soup into the cart.

While checking out at the store, Nicole startled him by saying, "It sounds like you two are getting really close. Does this mean you two are more than a vacation fling? Are you thinking about coming back to town again sometime?"

Nicole didn't pretend to protest when Maxwell swiped his credit card. Neither mentioned that her own wallet was still in the house, probably destroyed like so much of her other stuff. "I don't know. I mean yes, it's definitely turned into more than what we'd initially planned. We're going to give it a try, but I just don't know what any of that really will mean once I have to leave in a few days. I'm still active duty. It isn't like the Army is just gonna let me move back home because I'm falling for some amazing guy."

Nicole squeezed against his side in a comforting hug.

By the time they made it home, it was after two o'clock in the morning. Maxwell poked his head into the bedroom, but Brick was already asleep. Maxwell ached to join him and press his body against Brick's and try to steal some of the peace that seemed to be radiating off him.

First, he needed to get Nicole settled, though.

Maxwell showed her the spare room, and was getting ready to join Brick in his bed when she said, "Maxwell, I'm still scared. I'm afraid of... I'm just afraid, you know?"

Maxwell understood. He frequently had trouble sleeping after his more dangerous missions. On those nights, when he walked around the base, trying to wear himself out, he frequently saw some of his friends seemingly doing the same. Some wanted to be left alone with their own thoughts while others needed someone to talk to about sports, politics, their family back home, anything other than their mission.

"I get it. It'll take a while. What can I do to help tonight?"

"Can you stay in here with me until I fall asleep? I'm so tired, but I know sleep won't come if I'm alone."

Maxwell cast a longing glance across the hall to Brick's room. That was where he really wanted to be. He realized that he was a little shaken himself. But he wasn't going to wake Brick up. "Absolutely. I could use some company tonight too. Give me a second to change. When you get your jammies on, open the door and I'll come back in. We can share the bed tonight and talk until we fall asleep."

In the end, neither of them said much. But having somebody next to her helped Nicole fall asleep.

Maxwell listened to her breathing for a while longer before giving up on being able to find sleep without Brick's help. Moving ever so slowly, he crept out of Nicole's room, and quietly joined Brick. He was already sleeping, but just lying next to his body was enough for Maxwell to be able to finally fall asleep.

CHAPTER 24

Brick

A s he awoke, Brick stretched and yawned while wondering how Maxwell and Nicole were doing. The last he'd heard, Nicole seemed fine, but was being poked and prodded by the doctors. Maxwell had decided he was going to stay with her until she was released. Brick had offered to come wait with him, but Maxwell had said that Brick should rest up because he was going to jump him as soon as he made it home.

Brick smiled at the thought before realizing that if Maxwell hadn't come home yet, Nicole might have a problem.

He rolled toward the edge of his bed to reach for his phone

so he could check for messages, but received a pleasant surprise when he bumped into Maxwell's warm body lying beside him, instead. Forgetting all about his phone, Brick reached for Maxwell. His hand traced down Maxwell's hard body, slowly letting himself feel every ridge of his ridiculous abs before reaching down into his pajama pants to grab a hold of his morning erection.

Maxwell rolled from his side onto his back to give Brick better access, but his eyes were still closed and his breathing still completely even.

After everything he went through yesterday he deserves to wake up this morning with a bang.

Brick traced his finger over the tip of his cock and was rewarded with beads of moisture that he quickly used to lubricate the entire shaft, before starting to stroke his new lover. Just as he was starting to build up a good momentum, Maxwell groaned and arched his back.

"Good morning," Maxwell whispered with his eyes still closed, but a big, beautiful smile on his face.

Brick nibbled Maxwell's ear and said, "Good morning to you, too. You just lay there and let me do the work. I bet you a dollar I can make you scream."

When Brick started sliding under the blankets to give his boyfriend the perfect morning blowjob, Maxwell grabbed his shoulders, and pulled him back up to the top of the bed.

"What's the matter?" Brick asked. "Not in the mood for me

anymore? You're not exactly Prince Charming yourself, you know, you stink like hell." Brick joked, tickling Maxwell to let him know he was just kidding around.

Maxwell squirmed and shushed Brick until he stopped.

What the hell's going on?

Brick lay on his side with his head resting on his hand, staring at Maxwell. He was slightly disappointed at being stopped, but chalked it up to Maxwell just not being in the mood after all the shit from the night before.

I could certainly get used to waking up like this every morning, even without any sex.

Feeling like an ass, Brick realized that Maxwell probably wasn't in the mood because of what had happened with his friend. Before Maxwell had a chance to fall back asleep, Brick asked, "So how did everything go at the hospital?"

Maxwell rubbed the sleep from his eyes. "As good as can be expected. The house will have to get rebuilt completely. We got her out of there quickly enough that she's going to be fine. But they still don't know where Billy is."

"Shit. Did they put her up somewhere safe?"

"Kind of." Maxwell chuckled. "She's in the spare bedroom. They promised they would patrol the neighborhood and they're going to be increasing the search for Billy now that she's told them everything he did."

Knowing he was being petty, Brick was annoyed that Maxwell hadn't asked first before inviting Nicole to stay the night.

He would have agreed, of course, but it would have been nice to be asked since it *was* his house. Then he remembered that he hadn't checked his phone yet. There was probably a message on it from Maxwell asking just that.

Either way, it didn't matter.

No matter what had happened during the mess the night had turned into, all that mattered was they were all safe now.

Right? Why am I still bothered by this?

Maxwell broke the silence. "She was still a little freaked out last night so I stayed with her until she fell asleep. But I couldn't fall asleep, so I eventually made my way over here. That helped. Everything seems to calm down when I'm next to you."

Any annoyance faded away at the sweet words.

"Calms down? Around me?" He thought back to all the things that had happened since Maxwell had arrived. "Things must be really wild where you're from if this is calm."

Maxwell rolled to face Brick, and rubbed his hand over Brick's smooth chest, squeezing the muscles. "You know what I mean. Anyway thanks for rushing in to help me get her out. Neither of us would have made it without you. I'm plenty used to danger, but not fires, I guess. I was starting to panic before you appeared and snapped me out of it."

Brick nodded. "All's well that ends well. What's Nicole's long-term plan? Will her insurance put her up in a hotel or something while they rebuild her place?"

Brick felt bad as soon as the cold words left his mouth. He was struggling, though, trying to reconcile his need to maximize his time with Maxwell with his desire to help a stranger, who happened to be a friend of Maxwell's.

His need for Maxwell was winning, and Brick wasn't exactly happy about what that said about himself.

"I'm not sure," Maxwell said. "I told her she can stay here. So I'm not sure if she'll bother with the insurance for a little while. Well, the hotel part anyway."

Brick snapped at how casually Maxwell had decided that it was okay to let someone move into Brick's house. "So without even asking me, you invited a stranger to just stay in my house until she's ready to move out? What if she decides that she doesn't want to?"

The words sounded too harsh as soon as they'd left his mouth, but it was too late. Maxwell pulled his hand away from Brick's chest, leaving a cold emptiness behind.

"She's not a stranger, Brick. She's my friend. Just like you're my friend. I'm sure she'd help you if you needed it. But if it's gonna be too much for you, we'll move into a hotel today. But I can't just abandon her right now, you know?"

There was no way Brick was going to let Maxwell leave just because of the Nicole situation. Realizing how close he was to losing Maxwell, he pushed aside his own selfishness. Despite the fact that the two of them had just met a few days earlier, if Maxwell considered her a friend, Brick knew he should too.

That's what being in a relationship meant.

"Sorry, man. I'm being an ass. Of course she can stay. What's the point of having the spare room if not to let guests stay in it? We'll tell her she can stay as long as she needs to. Even after you're gone if she wants."

"Thank you, Brick. That means so much to me." His eyes went wide. "Crap. I'm so sorry. I just realized that I completely imposed on you like I own this place. Are you really okay with all of this? I can tell her that she needs to find somewhere else."

It was like a weight had been lifted from his chest. Simply hearing Maxwell ask rather than assuming meant the world to Brick. He wasn't just an afterthought to whatever Maxwell decided he wanted to do. They were partners going through it together.

"I am now. We'll help her get back on her feet."

Maxwell rolled on to Brick's chest and kissed him passionately to show just how much it meant. Just when Brick was wondering how big a reward he was about to get, Maxwell rolled off the bed and waved for Brick to follow him. "Come on, lazybones. Let's go tell her the good news."

Brick stretched one last time before getting out of bed. He couldn't help thinking that he was waking up to a whole new morning. Something big was changing in his life.

CHAPTER 25

Maxwell

ALL THREE SAT AROUND WATCHING TV for several hours, and ordering pizza for lunch when they got hungry. Everything started out amazingly. Maxwell couldn't believe how generous Brick was being with his house. He wasn't sure if he'd have reacted so gracefully if the tables were turned.

Nicole had talked to the police first thing in the morning, but as the day passed, Maxwell was growing frustrated that they hadn't found Billy yet.

As the afternoon lingered on, Brick seemed to fade, though.

If Maxwell wasn't mistaken, Brick sounded a little annoyed as he excused himself to go workout in the garage.

Hopefully, he's just tired. But I'll have to check on him later.

"Hey, can we go shopping again and pick up some more clothes before dinner?" Nicole asked during a quiet spot in the show.

"Sure. I'll go see if Brick wants to come, too."

Brick didn't look up when Maxwell walked into the garage.

"Hey, Brick, Nicole and I are going out to do some shopping. Why don't you come with us? It'll be fun. I think we could all use a little time out of the house."

Brick grunted and started a set of dumbbell curls without saying another word.

Maxwell sighed dramatically, but even that didn't earn a glance from Brick. Not used to not being the only one in a relationship that needed time alone, Maxwell wasn't sure what to do about Brick's mood.

Deciding that poking the bear might be the easiest way to get to the root of the problem and find a solution, he said, "What's up your butt, man? We need to have a little fun and Nicole needs more than one outfit. Let's multitask." Maxwell kept his voice light, even while growing more frustrated with Brick and embarrassed with himself for how often he'd given others exactly the same silent treatment.

"You forgot, didn't you?" Brick set the dumbbells on the ground and stood to adjust the weights on the bench press bar.

"Forgot what?" Maxwell asked, scouring his brain to remember what Brick was talking about.

"Chicago. We were supposed to go downtown to do some clubbing. It's fine, though. I'm not really in the mood anymore." Brick sat down on the bench, but instead of grabbing the bar he'd just prepared, he crossed his hands over his lap and stared blankly across the garage.

Shit. I thought that was tomorrow.

"I'm so sorry, man. It's just been so crazy that it slipped my mind. I definitely want to go. Please don't back out just because I'm stupid. We *have* to go dancing tonight. I can tell Nicole to either go without me or wait until tomorrow."

"You sure you're not just using this as an excuse to cool things off between us? If so, I get it. Just tell me, okay?" Brick fidgeted with the bar, looking sad and nervous.

"No way, Brick. I really forgot. I'm all in with us. You're going to have to pry me off with a spatula if you want to get rid of me."

Brick smiled and blew out a breath he must have been holding in. "Awesome. Hey, why don't you take her out and do that shopping. We have plenty of time before we need to leave. I'll finish working out. Take my car."

Maxwell straddled Brick's lap. He could feel Brick's smile while their kiss stretched on.

"We're definitely going to fool around later, right?" Maxwell said, wishing they didn't need to wait that long.

213

"Absolutely. Maybe we'll get a room downtown so we won't have to worry about how much noise we make," Brick whispered, his eyes darting to the door.

Nicole had just walked in. When she saw them, she covered her eyes and said, "Sorry. I just got here. I didn't see anything. Should I just go shopping by myself and leave you guys alone?"

Laughing, Brick said, "No. You two go and get what you need. Maxwell is too hot. He'd wear me out if I tried to hang around him all day, and we have plans for later."

"Oh, should I plan on spending the night somewhere else?" Nicole asked, sounding nearly as excited for them as Maxwell felt.

"No. I think we're going to plan on doing a little too much drinking and stay somewhere downtown." Brick said, squeezing Maxwell's butt.

Right in front of Nicole.

Maxwell thought back at how spooked he'd been by her appearing at the lighthouse. He couldn't believe how quickly things were changing.

* * *

Since neither had all that much money, they ended up at Target, figuring they'd get a fair amount of reasonable quality clothes without spending a ton. Nicole repeatedly tried to convince Maxwell that Goodwill would be fine, but he kept reminding her that she deserved some brand new replacement clothes.

While searching through the racks, Maxwell asked the question he'd been too afraid to ask earlier. "I hate to bring it up, but have you given any thought about where Billy could've gone? The cops will be following any lead we give them, so we can certainly help point them in the right direction."

Nicole turned away from the rack they were investigating and walked a few feet away, clearly not wanting to talk about Billy.

Maxwell left plenty of physical space between them, but pressed on. "I know it's scary to think about. But Billy needs to be locked up. He's clearly unstable. I mean what kind of guy burns down the shed, and then the house with his girlfriend tied up inside of it without some kind of problems? And it's clearly escalating, and you're the one who will get hurt."

Maxwell had his own thoughts about what would be a suitable punishment: Billy locked up in a small room with no windows, and Maxwell allowed in once a day to dish out daily beatings. He knew not to say any of that out loud, though. Even if she could admit that Billy was a dick, that didn't mean she didn't have feelings for him after all the time they'd been together.

Nicole surprised Maxwell by actually saying anything at all. "We were fighting. That's what happened with the shed. And then after that, I told him I was leaving him. I shouldn't have taken so much time to change the locks." She talked as if she had done something to justify him behaving like an animal. "I know he's a bad man, but I'm so scared of him. It's stupid, but I wish I could just ignore the problem and he'd go away."

Maxwell couldn't believe she had admitted so much. "The easiest way for the problem to die down is for him to get caught by the police. He has to have friends or family he could be holed up with. I think you should tell the police anything you know. I'll protect you until they find him." Maxwell flexed his biceps, trying to lighten the mood.

Nicole smiled at his silliness, but shook her head sadly. "You're only here for a few more days. What happens when you leave? We talked about that already. You can't protect me from all the way over in Afghanistan."

Maxwell had always been proud of his military service. He believed that every bad person that they caught or killed helped to protect innocent people around the world. It was a cruel irony that the same military service meant that he couldn't protect the one individual back in America that needed his protection most.

He pulled a red, stretchy dress off the rack and held it up to her while saying, "If we can help the cops, they can catch him quicker. If it takes longer than my time here, I bet Brick will take care of you. We can talk to him about a long-term plan when we get back."

She scrunched up her nose, clearly not wanting to talk about the Billy situation any more. Maxwell decided he'd bring it up again in a couple of days.

He shook the dress at Nicole. "Go try this on. You'll look cute."

She rolled her eyes at him. "That is so not my style. Besides I'm not really interested in impressing any guys anytime soon."

Maxwell knew her road to recovery would be a long one after the traumatic incident, but he was going to do his best to try and encourage her to not hide herself in a shell for too long. "I didn't say to wear it for a guy. There clearly aren't many guys that deserve what you have to offer. But you'll look pretty in it. Do it for yourself, not anyone else. I know I always feel better when I dress up a little. I absolutely love it when we have to wear our dress uniforms back on base."

When he pressed the dress into her hands, she didn't push it away, but she still didn't look convinced. He tried to close the deal. "Besides, I'll pay for the dress. After Brick and I get back from Chicago, you can do up your hair and put on a little makeup, and I'll take some pictures of you all dolled up. It'll be fun. It'll be like the makeover scene in *The Breakfast Club*."

Nicole squinted at Maxwell. "What's that?"

"Oh my God. Hurry up. Try this on, and pick out the rest of your clothes. Your job tonight is to watch that movie while we're gone. It's a classic and will change your life."

With new purpose, they rushed through the rest of their

shopping trip. Nicole agreed on the red dress, but wouldn't let Maxwell pay for it. Waving the credit card that had arrived in the mail earlier that morning, she said, "If I'm wearing it just for me, then I should be the one buying it."

Laughing and shouting, when they got home, they stormed in the front door of Brick's house and dumped their bags on the couch. Maxwell went to look for Brick to see if they were going to leave before or after dinner.

Brick was standing in the living room with a serious look on his face. "Don't kill me. Can we go to Chicago some other day?"

Maxwell felt the color drain from his face as he fell against the side of the doorframe, wondering what had happened to Brick's earlier excitement for their plan of spending time alone together.

Is he getting cold feet?

CHAPTER 26

Brick

"WHOA, HOLD ON." BRICK SAID, seeing the disappointment on Maxwell's face. "It's nothing like that. I still want to take you downtown and make a night of it. But there's a band coming to Chicago in two or three days. I heard a commercial on the radio when I was in the garage. One of my friends is in the band. I haven't seen him since he moved to Tennessee years ago, but it seems like they are doing pretty well. If it's okay, I'd like to check them out."

Maxwell nodded as a smile broke out on his face. "Sounds

like a blast. But you should have led with that and saved me a heart attack." Maxwell lightly punched Brick in the shoulder.

"Sorry." Brick pulled Maxwell close for a kiss that he hoped made up for it. "Hey, can I borrow your laptop to look up when and where they'll be?"

"Absolutely." Maxwell turned to Nicole. "Hey, we can watch the movie together now."

"What are you watching?" Brick asked while Maxwell walked to the table to open his laptop.

"The Breakfast Club. Do you want to watch with us?"

"Don't mess with the bull, young man. You'll get the horns." Brick said, making his hand into the head of a bull and shaking them at Maxwell.

"I take it that's a yes. You look up your friend, and we'll try to find out where we can stream it from."

Maxwell handed the laptop to Brick and raced through the house with Nicole right behind him.

Brick was happy that the change of plans hadn't upset Maxwell. Based on how excited the two of them were, staying home to watch the movie would probably prove to be a rowdy night.

Brick opened a tab on the browser and looked up the band. They were going to be in town in two days.

That should work out perfectly. Maybe I'll have a chance to make a reservation somewhere nice for dinner.

He closed his tab and found himself staring at Maxwell's

email. Even knowing that he was being an asshole for doing it, he couldn't stop from looking.

There was only one unread message. Brick gasped when he read the subject line.

Can't wait until vacation.

The sender was someone other than Brick. Despite Maxwell's assurances, it looked like he was still planning on going to see someone else soon.

He isn't coming back for Christmas.

Moving almost of their own accord, his fingers dragged the mouse pointer and clicked to open the email.

He only managed to catch the highlights as his anger boiled over.

> *I wish you were already here.*
> *I don't know how I'll wait until Christmas time.*
> *That picture you sent was so sexy, but can I get one where you're not wearing a shirt?*
> *If you're half as good in bed as you sound in email, I'm ordering delivery for the entire time you're here, and not letting you out of my bedroom. Unless you like fucking on the balcony. LOL.*

Brick couldn't believe what he was reading. Another man was talking to his boyfriend the same way Brick used to in his emails to Maxwell.

Boyfriend? Relationship? Ha. This whole thing's a sham.

Brick slammed the laptop shut without bothering to mark the email as unread. He was beyond caring about keeping Maxwell from finding out that he'd spied on him.

He wanted to run out of the house, or hide in the garage lifting weights. Instead, he decided that since *he* at least was serious about his feelings for Maxwell, he needed to stop running when things didn't go his way.

"Maxwell, can you come here for a minute?" he called, trying to hide his anger.

What did I expect? Our plan was for this to just be a fling. Who cares if he pretended that he wanted more just because it was what I wanted to hear. I'm the one who's changing the rules.

"What's up?" Maxwell asked, giving Brick a peck on the cheek before catching a hint that Brick was upset. "Hey, are you okay? Something happen to your friend?"

"I guess I don't need to buy you a Christmas present, right?" Brick asked, fighting really hard to not start yelling.

Maxwell squinted at Brick. "What are you talking about? Is this some kind of game?"

"Well, since you'll be with Darren, I figured he'd be the one that needed to shower you with presents."

"I don't understand...shit. How'd you find out about him?" Maxwell took a few steps back from Brick.

"You left your email open."

Maxwell sighed. "Listen. We had plans before I came out here. He had something for work come up so we rescheduled. That's how I had the time available to visit you. We should really be thanking him. But, there's nothing between us. I just haven't thought about him since we...became a thing."

Brick crossed his arms and stared at Maxwell, trying to read his face.

"Seriously. I don't want anyone else." Maxwell started typing on his laptop. "See. Come look."

Brick reluctantly joined Maxwell and looked where he pointed.

I've met someone else that I'm falling hard and fast for. I'm not going to be coming out for Christmas or ever. I'll be spending all my free time with the most incredible fireman ever. Take care.

"Is that better?" Maxwell asked.

"Yes. I just thought—"

"Of course you did," Maxwell said. "Why wouldn't you have? I don't blame you one bit. But that was the old me. That's just part of the baggage that I bring to the relationship. I'll work hard at being a better man for you."

The tension that Brick had been carrying in his shoulders disappeared, leaving Brick tired. He collapsed onto a kitchen chair. "I was so worried I was losing you already."

Maxwell sat on Brick's lap and gave him a kiss. "I'm not going anywhere. Well, except back to base, of course. I can't do anything about that. Do you still want to keep me around?"

"Shut up, dude. I don't want to think about *that* yet. But, yes. We'll work it out. Let's go watch the movie and enjoy the rest of the night."

They walked hand in hand to the TV room, but froze when they got there.

Nicole was staring at her phone. "That was the police. Someone called in a report that they saw Billy in the neighborhood."

Brick turned to look back down the hall while Maxwell rushed over to give her a hug.

"What are we going to do?" she asked.

Brick answered first. "We're going to make sure at least one of us is always with you. I think Billy's too big of a pussy to try anything while we're around."

Maxwell nodded. "We'll be here for you."

Hoping to avoid a night where they all jumped at shadows, Brick said, "So, I heard we were watching a movie tonight. Should I make some popcorn?"

CHAPTER 27

Maxwell

*J*UST BEFORE NICOLE WALKED OUT the front door the next morning to ride with the police officer who had come to pick her up, she pointed at Maxwell and Brick and said, "So, they say this should take a couple hours. I'll make sure I'm very chatty and stretch it out to three. For those of you playing along at home, that's a lot of time for you to get into plenty of fun trouble. Don't let me down."

Maxwell said, "Oh my God, Nicole. Do you *not* have a filter?"

But he wasn't really mad. Especially when he felt Brick's hand on his back. He leaned against Brick and was rewarded by

Brick draping his arm over his shoulder like a warm, well-muscled blanket and started making plans about how to spend the time with Brick.

"Call us if you need anything," Brick said, gently nudging her out the door and locking it behind her.

As soon as the police car pulled out of the driveway, Brick pinned Maxwell against the wall and smothered him with passionate kisses. Maxwell nearly gave in to his lust and followed wherever Brick wanted to lead. But there were a couple specific things he wanted to do and they'd run out of time if he didn't stand strong right away.

"Whoa, there, cowboy," Maxwell said, dropping down beneath his arms to escape. "We've got three hours here. No sense rushing anything."

Brick leaned his back against the wall, looking like he was trying to appear casual while his words told a different story. "You're killing me, man. If there's one thing I've learned since you've been here, it's that we have to take advantage of any moment we get or we're going to get interrupted."

Brick leaned in for another kiss, but Maxwell pushed against his chest to hold him off. "But don't you want to hear my plan, at least?"

Groaning, but clearly not upset, Brick said, "Sure. But here's my plan. Fuck and then fuck some more. So whatever you're offering has got to be better than that."

"I was thinking we could take some of this time we have and get naked. I could get the camera—"

Brick interrupted. "No, no, no. I couldn't do that. I'd be way too embarrassed."

Maxwell nodded, a little surprised at Brick's change of heart on the subject. "Okay. That's fine. I won't push you. I was just thinking that it might be fun and sexy to take the photos today. Kind of foreplay. But then when we're separated later, and feeling lonely and frustrated, we'd have the pictures of each other to help...inspire us."

Brick's eyes went wide and his mouth made a cute O shape. "Ah. Well, perhaps I was a little hasty."

Knowing that he'd already won the battle, Maxwell decided to win the war, too. He pressed his body against Brick's, feeling his boyfriend's already-hard cock against his stomach. It took all of his willpower to resist dropping down onto his knees and unzipping Brick's pants. "But since you said you couldn't and that you just wanted to go fuck, I say we get our dicks ready and get right to the hot-and-heavy fucking."

Maxwell watched Brick swallow as he took a second to make up his mind. "I'm not changing my mind about wanting the fucking. But you make a solid point about how useful taking a few minutes now to take some sexy photos might be to us later. So let's give your suggestion a try. We'll call it a compromise."

Maxwell hurried off to grab his camera. When he returned, Brick was already naked. "Wow. When you make up your mind about something, you really make up your mind, huh?"

When Brick flexed his enormous biceps, Maxwell forgot what he'd been talking about.

"I try," Brick replied. "Deciding what I wanted worked out well with you. I'm not even worried about our time apart anymore. I mean, it's going to suck, of course, but I've committed myself to believing that we're in this for the long haul, so I'm not worried about it not working out. We won't let it."

Maxwell snapped a picture. "I'm doing my best not to worry, but I don't have the best track record with relationships. If you ever see me pulling away, just remind me that I'm not my dad."

Brick turned to show off his back for the camera. "That seems pretty obvious. Do you want to talk about it a little bit so I know what to watch out for?"

Maxwell knew that the only way he'd ever be able to truly get over his dad would be to learn to talk through how he felt about him. Until Brick, he'd never had anyone he'd wanted to share something so personal with. With Brick, Maxwell thought he might finally be strong enough to stop using his dad as a crutch and thrive in a relationship for once.

It would all start with being able to open up about how he'd been affected by what his dad had done. It would mean admitting that he'd not been strong enough to prevent letting his dad have that kind of power over him.

"He had an affair when I was in high school. Well, he got caught for *that* affair. He'd had plenty prior, we found out later."

"I'm sorry, man. So he left?" Brick had stopped flexing.

Maxwell nodded, forgetting all about his camera. "Yeah. Mom even tried to forgive him and move forward. For my sake, I think. But once he'd been busted, something changed in him. He didn't want us anymore. He got cruel and weird. He'd disappear for a month and then pop back in for a couple days. Usually around his birthday or a holiday. And then he'd be gone again just when it seemed like he might be making an attempt. He kept tearing me and Mom's wounds open repeatedly, with longer breaks between visits."

"So that's why you never go back to a place you vacation at?"

Maxwell smiled sadly. "I guess. I figure that if they want me more than I want them, it would be more rude to keep showing up a couple times a year, expecting them to halt the rest of their life to spend time with me. I don't know, it's stupid. I'm just afraid that I'll turn into my dad."

Maxwell wanted Brick to say something to show that everything was going to be okay. But he also knew that he was by far more likely to be the reason if it wasn't. "There's one big difference with you, though, that I think might make this all different with us."

"What's that?" Brick said in a near whisper.

"I like you more than you like me. I need you like air and food and water. There's no way I'll ever not want to hurry back any chance I get."

Smiling, Brick said, "Well, that's nice of you to say, but you're wrong, of course. You can't want me more than I want you. That's impossible. That's the real difference with us. We *both* want this. We belong together. But, I promise to keep my eyes open and call you out if you start looking like you're slipping away. "

Maxwell aimed the camera at Brick again and zoomed in on his dick. "Thank you. Now turn to the side so I can get a good picture of just how long that dick of yours is."

Brick, with his hands on his hips, obeyed Maxwell's request. "You almost done there? Because you look entirely over-dressed and, from what I can tell, you're the only one that'll be getting any pictures to keep out of this."

"Well, I had an idea about that," Maxwell said. His heart raced at the possibility that Brick might agree.

"Uh oh. Based on your face, I'm guessing this is going to be a wild one."

Maxwell nodded. "Here's what I propose. I get naked. We move to your room. And then we'll take some pictures of me fucking you."

Brick laughed, but his expression turned serious when Maxwell nodded. "Whoa. You're not joking."

Maxwell let the camera rest against his chest. "Sorry. Too much, too fast?"

"Probably. But, damn, you made that prostate thing sound so intense the other night. I've gotta know what that's like. What the fuck. Let's do it."

Maxwell's heart skipped a beat. He hadn't expected Brick to actually agree. Most of the men he'd been with had either only wanted to give or receive, not both. As much as he loved feeling Brick's dick in his ass, Maxwell had hoped that it wasn't going to mean a lifetime of never getting to return the favor.

"Hurry up, man. My curiosity is piqued. Let's get this party started."

While Maxwell had been lost in his thoughts, Brick had made his way down the hall and was waiting in the bedroom doorway.

"I'm coming," Maxwell said picking up his camera bag to make sure he had any equipment they might need.

"Hopefully not too fast," Brick said, disappearing into the bedroom.

CHAPTER 28

Brick

THE FIRST THING BRICK DID when Maxwell made his way down the hall was pull him into the room, shut the door behind him, and click the lock button.

"She's not going to suddenly pop up on us this time," Brick said. The camera was going to be intimidating enough. There was no way he'd survive if Nicole walked in on them during their lovemaking.

Brick grabbed the bottom of Maxwell's shirt and pulled it off over his head. He traced the tattoo shaped like a rainbow on his left pec and then the pixelated Zelda tattoo on his right.

"We should get you a tat next time I come home," Maxwell said.

"I'm not agreeing to anything when I'm this horny. There's no way that ends well for me," Brick said, pinching Maxwell's nipple and getting the moan he'd been hoping to hear.

"Well, I was going to say that you should lay down on the bed and let me suck your dick for a few minutes, but I guess you won't want to do that either." Maxwell squeezed Brick's dick. What *would* you like to do?"

Brick jumped onto the bed and rolled onto his back. "Well, as luck would have it, I'd like to lay down on this bed and let you suck my cock."

"That sounds like a great idea. I'm glad you thought of it." Maxwell handed the camera to Brick. "Here. Why don't you try to get some good pics to remember me by while I'm down there."

Brick almost dropped the camera when Maxwell wrapped his mouth around his dick and started sucking on the tip while looking Brick directly in the eyes, hypnotizing him for a few seconds until Brick realized that Maxwell's mouth wasn't moving.

"Everything okay down there?" Brick asked.

Maxwell pulled his mouth away and started stroking Brick's cock vigorously. His hand squeezed with the perfect amount of tightness. Brick arched his back like a puppet being dragged around by its strings.

"Everything's fine. But if I'm moving, the pictures will turn out blurry. Let's try that again."

Brick wanted to yell at Maxwell when he pulled his amazingly active hand off his dick and replaced it with his mouth that didn't move and those eyes that reached right into his soul and threatened to tear Brick in two.

Right. Pictures.

Looking at the display, Brick saw Maxwell's mouth wrapped around his dick in an entirely new way. Somehow it was so much more visual than just seeing it through his own eyes. It was also a million times more taboo and sexy.

He snapped a picture.

"Okay, Maxwell. Now take more of me into your mouth. As much as you can."

Maxwell didn't hesitate.

"Fuck, that's hot as hell." He continued snapping pictures as Maxwell kissed and nibbled and sucked on him from the tip all the way down to his balls, and then further back.

"Oh. That's...wow." Brick couldn't focus on the sensations shooting across his body and the camera, so he gave up on the camera, figuring there was no way he'd ever forget the moment.

With each flick of Maxwell's tongue, the jolts got stronger until Brick finally reached his ultimate destination.

Brick reached to his left to pull open the bedside table. Grabbing the lube and condoms, he threw them all down to

Maxwell. "Here. I want more. I need you inside me. Work your magic."

Maxwell was generous with the lube.

Knowing what was coming next, Brick laid his head back and relaxed his body. It came easy around Maxwell. Brick trusted him completely. The two had been through so much together. They'd literally laid their lives on the line when the other needed help.

Maxwell started with one finger, and quickly was able to add a second. Brick tried to focus on the new feelings. He supposed it was nice, but it just made him feel filled up. It was intense being possessed so completely by Maxwell, but there was no magical physical sensation.

Maybe it doesn't work for all guys.

When it actually started getting slightly uncomfortable, like Maxwell's fingers weren't exactly where they belonged, Brick took a couple deep breaths to see if it would pass and was about to ask Maxwell to stop when the feeling started to change. A gentle buzzing started in his core.

When Brick let out a whimper, Maxwell pressed a little harder. The buzzing grew and spread down his legs.

"Damn. I think you found it," Brick said, happy that he'd managed to avoid drooling on himself.

The sense of being manhandled was much stronger than with anything they'd done before. Maxwell was in charge, and Brick liked it. He'd return the favor later, but for now, it felt great to lie back and let Maxwell decide exactly how Brick should be pleasured.

"Trust me. I know I found it." Maxwell had a serious look on his face. "Now let's get to the real fun. Give me the camera."

Brick felt empty and exposed when Maxwell removed his fingers and reached for the camera. Brick wasn't sure they needed any more photos, but he trusted Maxwell to make it worth their while.

Maxwell walked across the room and set the camera on a dresser. He looked at the display and shifted the camera around until he was happy with it. Where it was sitting, it would have a side view of the two men.

Without another word, Maxwell picked up a condom, tore into the wrapper, unrolled it over his ready dick, and climbed onto the bed.

Brick had never really thought about being fucked before. The couple times he'd had sex prior to Maxwell, he'd always been on top. He liked the top. But as Maxwell approached, and Brick remembered what his fingers had done to him, Brick knew he would never want to *only* be on top ever again.

"What about the camera? I thought we were going to get some pictures." Brick asked.

"I'm one step ahead of you. It's recording as we speak. Wave at the camera," Maxwell said while he took a second to wave at it.

"You serious?" Brick asked. Still photos were one thing. But video, well that was porno. "I don't know if I can do this, man. I mean, videos are different."

"I know. They're more raw and intimate. And way fucking hotter. That's why you were jacking off to a video instead of a magazine when I first showed up, right?"

Brick laughed, blushing at the memory.

"Hey," Maxwell said, comfortingly. "Nothing to be embarrassed about. We all do it. But why not do it while watching ourselves...well, do it. Right?"

Brick immediately nodded. "That's a great idea. Insane, but great. Fuck me, Maxwell Cope."

Maxwell didn't hesitate. He gently, but firmly pushed into Brick.

His fingers had only been a tease for what it felt like to be filled. It was like Maxwell had taken the dial and spun it up to eleven.

Brick wanted Maxwell to start thrusting, but he was taking his time instead, shifting his hips to slightly adjust his angle until Brick felt that familiar pressure again and gasped.

"Ah, there we are. You ready for me?"

"Now and forever," Brick said, wrapping his hands around Maxwell's forearms.

Those appeared to be the magic words. Maxwell thrust, starting in short, easy strokes, and very slowly upping the pace until the slap of their bodies echoed through the room.

Maxwell grunted and called out Brick's name.

Brick knew he'd rewatch those moments.

Brick wanted one more thing for the time when they would have to be apart. "Look at the camera for me, Maxwell."

"Ha. You're catching on quickly," Maxwell said.

"Quick, man. I'm close."

Maxwell turned to look into the camera, smiled, and said, "I love you, Brick."

The words, and knowing he'd be able to watch them forever, undid Brick. He came so hard that he wasn't sure he'd ever stop. Maxwell continued fucking him, setting off repeated aftershocks.

Maxwell finished with one final smack of bodies, and his back arched as he unleashed into the condom.

"That's gonna be a fucking awesome video, Brick. You are one sexy man."

Everything made Brick giggle in the afterglow. "Oh my God. Turn off the camera. Hurry. Hurry."

When Maxwell returned to the bed, the two men lay cuddled against each other.

"I love you too, Maxwell."

"I thought you were going to leave me hanging," Maxwell joked.

"Man, that's just crazy. Every guy should know what that feels like. Those poor straight guys," Brick said, knowing that he sounded loopy.

"I think some of them are into it, but I know, right. Versatile's the only way to be."

Gaps started to stretch between their words as they both started getting sleepy.

At one point, Brick said, "Hey, why don't you go out with Nicole today? Make sure she's feeling okay after dealing with the cops."

"You sure?" Maxwell asked. "Shouldn't we spend the time together, just the two of us?"

"I think it'll be good for her. Besides, I'll just go watch a game with the guys, and then we'll meet up for dinner. You and me. We'll get some fancy desserts."

Maxwell rolled Brick to his side and spooned his back. After kissing his neck, he said, "You're all the dessert, I need."

"I was thinking ice cream," Brick said, threading his fingers through Maxwell's.

"Damn. You know everything I need, don't you?" Maxwell asked, his eyes starting to droop.

"I do my best."

They didn't get a chance to fall asleep, though. The front door opened and Nicole yelled, "I'm back. They wouldn't let me stay there forever. Put on some pants and come talk to me."

CHAPTER 29

Maxwell

AXWELL LOOKED AT THE MICROWAVE clock. It was nice being alone with Nicole, but he couldn't believe how much he missed Brick already. The afternoon was passing impossibly slowly. With only three more days left until his flight back, he was going to make sure that he spent every second with Brick once he came back home.

How will I survive until Christmas back in Afghanistan without him?

He filed that thought away as a problem for another day and clicked another file on his computer. He'd finished eleven months of the calendar and loved the pictures he'd created for each month.

He was still having trouble with September, though, which was Brick's month. Brick looked perfect in each one...almost. Maxwell was frustrated at his inability to capture some essence of Brick that was missing in the photos. No matter how much he fiddled with the color balances or tweaked the lighting, something just felt off.

I need to take a class if I'm going to continue working with great models like Brick and the other firefighters.

With a sigh, Maxwell started scrolling back through all of the photos he'd taken of Brick since arriving into town, hoping to find something that would work well enough. If he had time, he'd push for another photoshoot with Brick.

Somewhere private.

His dick responded by starting to get hard, agreeing that more private and intimate photos were just what they needed.

Maxwell was working on the light levels on one that was close to acceptable, when two hands snuck up from behind him and covered his eyes.

He recognized the voice immediately when Nicole asked, "Guess who?"

He'd nearly panicked in the first instant, thinking that Billy had broken into the home.

They need to catch that motherfucker before we all go crazy.

Nicole chased away the bad thoughts. She still brought a smile to Maxwell's face every time he saw her. She was an unexpected bright spot of the vacation.

"Any news about Billy?" Maxwell asked, stretching his back.

"No. Sounds like they think the sighting last night was a false alarm. They still don't have any clue where he is. They've checked all the spots I told them, and they'll have someone drive by every couple of hours. The whole thing sucks."

"Don't worry about it. I'm here for you." He couldn't help looking out the window.

"Where's Brick?" Nicole asked, pulling a chair around to his side of the table to sit next to him and stare at his laptop.

"He wanted me to spend some time with you today before he takes me out to dinner tonight. Do you think you'll be okay alone for a couple hours?"

Nicole stifled a yawn. "Yeah. I'll be good. I'm going to have to start doing it again sometime, right? For all I know, Billy's run off and moved to Vegas. At some point, I'll have to get used to living my life without worrying he's going to pop up. I'll try to catch up on some sleep while you're gone. Maybe see if I can figure out how to make it through more than a couple hours without waking up. Wanna go to the movies?"

"Absolutely. We'll find some mindless comedy and laugh and eat popcorn."

"Perfect. What are you working on there? Oh, sexy firemen pictures. How's the calendar coming?"

With no small amount of pride, Maxwell opened the eleven pictures he'd finished for the project. They both spent a half hour gawking at the handsome men, and joking about how everyone was wearing entirely too many clothes even in the pictures where they were just standing around in their shorts.

"Damn, we have some fine firemen in this area." Nicole said. "How did I not know this before?"

Maxwell opened the best picture he had of Brick, clicked the settings a couple of times, and surrendered to the fact that he would never be able to fix the shadows to his liking.

Nicole leaned in to give him a hug when he sighed. "The picture is amazing. You're just biased because you're in love."

Maxwell blushed. It was true, but the thought still scared the hell out of him.

"I'm so happy for you guys." She leaned against his arm. Despite her words, she seemed so very sad. "Hey, let's go watch that movie. I need some laughs right now."

Maxwell closed the laptop, perfectly happy to get to the movie so they could get back. He already missed being with Brick so badly.

Each minute away from Brick was killing him.

CHAPTER 30

Brick

Maxwell still wasn't home from the movie. Brick had left Clay and Ezra's after the sixth inning when they'd gotten tired of him being fidgety and constantly yelling at the pitchers to stop wasting so much time between pitches.

Excited about it getting closer and closer to time for their dinner date, but nervous and bursting with energy, Brick started cleaning the house to help pass the time. Now that he knew that Maxwell was going to talk to Nicole about cleaning up her stuff, Brick was happy to help her get started. Other than her messes, she'd quickly grown on Brick. She was a bizarre, funny woman when she had a moment to loosen up.

Brick hoped to get to know her better once Maxwell had to go back to the Army. Maybe they could plan a get-together every couple of weeks at the coffee shop and tell stories about Maxwell to each other.

He gathered all the clothes that Nicole had left all around the house, and set them on her bed. He did his best to sort the clean from the dirty, but as far as he was concerned once it had been left on the floor, it was dirty whether she'd worn it or not.

Not that I'm gonna judge.

With the floors cleared again, he was working on vacuuming the house while listening to music blasting through his headphones. He was trying some music Maxwell had suggested. Brick doubted that he would ever like it no matter how many more times he tried, but at least he'd be able to tell Maxwell he'd given dubstep a try.

He promised himself that once he'd made it through vacuuming, he'd switch to some good old-fashioned rock and roll before heading to clean the bathroom.

Brick hoped they'd get home soon so he'd be able to put off cleaning the bathroom for one more day. As much as he loved a clean house, he was much more interested in talking to Maxwell at the restaurant, and then coming home and locking the bedroom door and turning the radio on to cover any noises they might make.

He realized he'd been standing in one spot, imagining Maxwell on his knees with Brick's dick in his mouth. Telling himself to get back to work, he adjusted himself and cursed Maxwell's ability to get him all horny without even being in the house.

As soon as he reached out to grab the vacuum to finish the hall, something hit him in the back of the head. Pain exploded across his head in the split second before he started to black out and fall to the ground.

He had no idea how much time had passed when he came to. The headache was so bad when he first opened his eyes that he couldn't even keep them open. He groaned and tried to get to his feet, but fell back to the floor before getting too far.

He shook his head, trying to figure out what had happened and noticed a familiar smell.

Fire!

His headache mostly forgotten in the panic, Brick opened his eyes and saw Billy leaning against the back of the living room chair, smiling down at him.

"I'm so glad you woke up before I had to leave." He swung a baseball bat slowly through the air. "You big bastards sure are hard to take down. Good thing you were listening to that shitty music or I might not have been able to take you so easily.

Seriously? Dubstep? Haven't you heard that stuff will kill you?" Billy cackled, crazily.

Struggling to get to his feet, he realized that his ankles and knees were bound, as were his hands, which were tied behind his back. From his vulnerable position, he could see that the fire was roaring through the house.

Brick didn't let himself think about what would happen if help didn't come soon.

"Where's Nicki?" Billy asked, tapping Brick on the shoulder with the baseball bat.

"I don't know." Brick said, glad that he wouldn't have to try and lie. There was no way Billy was going to take him at his word, and Brick didn't really trust himself to not tell if Billy was crazy enough to stick around and continue to hurt him.

Not knowing didn't mean that he wasn't going to take the chance to needle Billy. After all, the odds of him not killing Brick no matter what Brick did seemed slim. "She flew to California to get away from your dumb ass."

Brick's smart mouth earned him a swift kick in the side from Billy. "It doesn't really matter where she's at, dumbass." Billy smiled as if repeating Brick's insult was witty. "I'll find her. I have all the time in the world, unlike you."

Brick continued struggling to free himself while Billy knelt down without an ounce of concern showing on his face. "I miss Nicole. I'm going to get her back, dipshit. It's like I'm not myself without her. She completes me, and calms the dark beast that's always trying to escape."

Brick was surprised at seeing any amount of tenderness from Billy, but then the psycho cackled again, and added, "I'll never let anyone else have her."

While he continued his crazy laughing, Brick wondered if the jealous thoughts that he'd had about Maxwell and his other lover would sound so creepy if he'd said them out loud. "You know what, Billy? I feel that same way about Maxwell. I got all jealous and pissed off the other day because I heard that another man was interested in him. "

Before Maxwell could continue, Billy kicked him in the side again. "Shut up. I don't wanna listen to any of that gay shit. You sick fucks creep me out."

Brick would have laughed if he didn't hurt so badly. The thought of anything being creepier than Billy was almost too much to imagine, and certainly the way Brick felt about Maxwell was nowhere in that vicinity.

Choking on the smoke, Brick continued, "The difference is that if he wants to go away, I'll let him. I won't be happy about it. I'll beg him to stay. But I love him enough that him being happy is more important than him being with me. Corny, right?"

Brick braced his body for the baseball bat, but instead Billy backed up, looking as if Brick were contagious.

Looking around at the fire, Billy regained his composure

and smiled at Brick. "Shit. It's getting pretty bad in here. This doesn't look safe at all. I think I'll go out to the front yard and watch from there until I hear the sirens. Feel free to scream for help. It'll be music to my ears and I'll bet it won't make one damn bit of difference in whether you get help or not."

Billy turned, and whistling a happy tune, walked out the front door, leaving Brick trapped all alone in the fire.

I've always had nightmares of dying in a fire, but I don't think I'm going to wake up and find out this was a dream this time.

As the fire continued to burn through the house, Brick just hoped that if he died, someone else would find him before Maxwell. He didn't want Maxwell to see him this way.

CHAPTER 31

Maxwell

W HEN THEY TURNED THE CORNER, the smoke, billowing out from the fire, interrupted the song Maxwell and Nicole had been singing while walking home.

"Jesus fucking Christ! This town is insane!" Maxwell yelled when he realized that the fire was at Brick's house. As he hit 9-1-1 on his phone, he corrected himself.

It's not the town, it's just Billy.

There was no way anyone or anything else had started the fire.

The operator answered the phone and asked what the

problem was. Before Maxwell could reply, he saw the evil psychopath standing in the front yard, casual as could be, watching the fire.

He handed his phone to Nicole and ran toward Billy. "I'm going to kill you, you motherfucker!"

Billy turned and smiled as if they were just two people crossing paths on the riverwalk. "Careful. Your boyfriend is burning alive in there...at least I think he's still alive. You probably shouldn't waste any of your time out here with me when he's in so much trouble."

What the hell happened while I was gone?

Not that it mattered. Brick was inside and needed Maxwell's help. Anything else was irrelevant.

He started running toward the house and made it to the first step when Billy laughed and shouted, "But surely you won't leave me alone with Nicki out here in the front yard!" Billy took a practice swing and smiled at Maxwell.

Billy started walking toward where Nicole stood frozen like a deer caught in headlights. She should have run and screamed. Instead she panicked and started slowly backing up with her hands held out in front of her.

Maxwell was trapped between two horrible choices.

For all he knew, Brick wasn't even inside the house. He could easily still be out with his friends or...Maxwell didn't want to consider it, but he knew there was a real chance that Brick was already dead and rushing in to save him would mean

Billy could do whatever he wanted to Nicole. Based on the way he was carrying the baseball bat, Maxwell didn't think that Billy intended to apologize to her about the things he'd done.

Looking proud of the trap he'd set, Billy turned to gloat to Maxwell. "The tough soldier and the big fucking fireman couldn't outsmart Billy, could you?"

Maxwell saw Nicole moving out of the corner of his eye, but ignored her entirely. Maxwell just hoped she'd run while Billy was distracted.

Instead, she seemed to be moving closer.

This isn't the time to try to talk sense into him. Run!

Maxwell moved into a ready crouch, hoping to distract him for long enough for Nicole to come to her senses.

Billy suddenly dropped the baseball bat and collapsed to the ground, unconscious.

Nicole stood behind him with a decent-sized rock held above her head.

"Nice job," Maxwell said, still trying to figure out what had just happened.

Nicole picked up the bat and yelled. "I've got him under control. Go get Brick."

Nicole had the bat, and she looked pissed as hell. She'd be able to take care of her ex while Maxwell checked the house to see if Brick was even there.

He better be okay, or I'll kill you, Billy.

When he turned back to the house, the fire had gotten

worse. Without taking another moment to make sure he was making the right decision, just knowing he needed to make a choice, he followed what his heart told him to do, and ran into his second fire in a week.

The smoke made seeing anything difficult, but Maxwell heard Brick's scream and followed it to the source.

"I can't believe you came back for me," Brick said.

Maxwell nearly cried with joy and screamed with rage when he saw Brick. He was tied up and left to die.

I should have been here to keep him safe. We all should have stuck together until Billy was in jail.

He helped Brick into a sitting position to make him easier to drag. "Of course, I came back for you. I don't ever plan on being away any longer than I need to anymore. I just can't believe you let yourself get caught by Billy, though. What's up with that?" Maxwell knew he'd have to confess to his own problems with Billy and how Nicole had saved him.

"Well, I had my headphones on—"

"Tell me once we're outside," Maxwell said.

As he dragged Brick through the door, Maxwell couldn't believe the luck that had brought him back from the movie theater earlier than he'd planned.

While struggling to get Brick off the porch, he heard sirens approaching. "Emergency crews sure do have a bad habit of getting here just a few seconds too late around here."

"We do the best we can. We may not get there as fast as

everybody wants, but we normally get there in time to do our job."

Maxwell was just about to point out that it sure would have been nice to have a few helpers carry Brick out of the house when he saw Billy move.

Nicole, reacting to the sirens, dropped the bat and turned to watch the cops as they pulled in the driveway. The fire truck stopped on the side of the street. Relieved that help had arrived, she waved at them excitedly.

Seeing Nicole with her back to him, Billy moved quickly to pick up the baseball bat and scramble to his feet. Lifting the bat high above his head, he prepared to swing it down at Nicole's head.

Maxwell drew a breath to warn Nicole to turn around, but he never got a chance to get the words out.

Billy never got a chance to finish the swing, either. A couple bullets hit Billy in the legs faster than Maxwell could blink. Billy backpedaled and dropped the bat as he fell to his ass, screaming in pain.

Two cops rushed forward. One keeping his gun aimed at Billy and yelling at him to stay on the ground. The other placing a knee in Billy's back to hold him in place while applying the handcuffs.

Billy continued to howl, but he almost seemed more mad that his plan hadn't worked than howling in actual pain.

Maxwell didn't even feel bad about thinking that the

screams were music to his ears. Billy deserved every ounce of pain or frustration anyone would ever give him for the rest of his life.

The cops swarmed around Billy, shouting commands for him to get on his stomach while they cuffed him.

Maxwell collapsed onto Brick once he was certain that everybody was going to be okay.

Blocking out the commotion of the police officers behind him, he took a moment to say, "I love you, Brick."

Each time he said the words, they rolled off his tongue more easily. He just hoped that he'd say it after fun times rather than when one of them nearly died going forward.

Brick kissed him back without any sign of hesitation. "I love you, too."

A second later Nicole joined the dog pile. "That was so intense, you guys. Just like a movie."

The three laughed, and turned to watch Billy getting dragged onto a stretcher, and put into the ambulance. A police officer climbed in after them, too. Maxwell was pretty sure that Billy would have plenty of time to get comfortable being around cops.

"I think that's going to take care of our Billy problem for a while," Nicole said.

CHAPTER 32

Brick

*A*FTER ASKING THEM A MILLION questions to gather any information they could about what exactly had happened at the house, and making them promise to come into the station to answer more the next day, the police left them alone to figure out exactly how to move on with their lives.

Before the ambulance left, the paramedics examined Brick and Maxwell. Neither wanted to go to the hospital and the paramedics eventually agreed that they were probably fine. Brick promised to take an aspirin for the headache, but it was already getting a lot better.

"They don't call me Brick for nothing," he joked before the paramedics climbed back in the ambulance and drove away.

The fire department was still working on putting out the fire. As he watched, Brick couldn't believe he was looking at his own house. The cleanup was going to be extensive, if it could even be done without just knocking it down and starting over.

Standing together in the front yard, Nicole broke the tension by saying, "I'd let you stay at my place, but, well...we'd have to buy some tents first."

Brick hugged her tightly, and rubbed her hair. "I'd let you stay at *my* place, but I'm having a little remodeling done. The place is a mess."

"I'd let you stay at *my* place," Maxwell added, "but the commute's a real bitch."

"It sounds like we need a hotel with some empty rooms," Brick suggested.

He was surprised about how little what had happened to the house bothered him.

It's just a place. Hell, it was just my place from back when I was alone. Now I've got Maxwell, and we're together. The rest will work itself out.

"I'll bunk with you," Maxwell said, standing on his tiptoes to give Brick a quick kiss.

Nicole stuck a finger in her mouth. "Gag me. I'll stay in my own room."

Brick clapped his hands together once, deciding that if

they stood around in the front yard long enough, he might come to his senses and feel bad about the house. "Two rooms it is. Let's go to the nice one up the river. My treat."

With one look back at the smoldering remains, they all climbed into Brick's car.

When they arrived at the hotel, Nicole was very adamant that her room should be on the opposite side of the building to make sure she didn't hear any of the goings-on in their room.

The young woman working the desk shrugged, and did her best to ignore their horseplay while she keyed in their information.

Brick couldn't believe how quickly all of them were able to find any reason for having fun so soon after the attack. They were probably in some kind of adrenaline spike. Brick worried about the crash, but at least he'd go through it with Maxwell. Based on how many times Maxwell had touched his arm, grabbed his hand, and even squeezed his butt while waiting at the counter, it looked like they were going to be perfect for helping each other through their recoveries.

"Hey, Nicole," Brick called out as they took their keycards and headed opposite ways. "If you need to talk, or just need people to sit near you, just call or knock on the door. Seriously. We're all in this together."

"Don't worry about me," she replied throwing up a peace sign with her fingers. "Between HBO and the porn channels, I'll be fine. You did say you were paying, right? I'll make sure to watch the expensive stuff first. Whoever wakes up first should wake the others so we can get some breakfast, though. Have fun, hot dudes." She blew them a kiss, and continued to her room.

"That girl's a trip," Brick told Maxwell.

"Yep. She'll be fine," Maxwell said, grabbing Brick's ass again. "But you look like you have some tension in your shoulders that you might need help with." Maxwell waved the keycard at Brick and started walking backward down the hall, luring Brick to follow him.

"You think my shoulders are tense. You should see my cock." As if it had just been waiting to hear its name, his dick *did* respond to their banter. The adrenaline hadn't come close to wearing off yet.

"I'm trying, big guy," Maxwell said. "You're the one getting hard and standing around in the middle of the lobby instead of rushing off to our room."

When they heard the woman at the desk clear her throat, they blushed and offered a quick, giggling apology before chasing each other up the stairs.

Brick whistled when they entered their room, impressed by the dark woods and the giant flat-screen monitor on the wall. The king-size bed had a white, fluffy blanket on it that gave Brick just one more reason to want to dive straight in. "I've heard about this place, but haven't ever been here. What's the point of staying at a hotel so close to home, right?"

"Sure. That'd be a waste of money." Maxwell grabbed the ice bucket from the bathroom counter. "Hey, let's get some ice and pop from the vending machines down the hall."

"No way," Brick said, locking the deadbolt. "You promised to give me a hand, and I need it now even more than ever."

Maxwell took a step back for each step that Brick took forward, but he couldn't hide the smile on his face. "Are you sure it's a hand that you want?"

"I want your hand, your mouth, and that tight ass of yours." Brick wasn't in the mood for playing too many games. He had some throbbing needs. If anything, the insane day had left him twice as horny as he usually was around Maxwell.

Maxwell turned and, with his feet flat on the ground, and his legs locked straight, bent forward and placed his chest submissively on the bed. "Like this."

"I'm not sure how I'll make use of your hands and mouth like that, but fuck yeah. That'll do nicely. We'll save using our hands and mouths and ice cubes and whatever else you think up for later tonight when we're ready to go again."

Brick stepped up behind Maxwell, and ground his dick against Maxwell's ass, cursing the jeans they were both still wearing.

"Hey, Brick, I meant what I said earlier. I love you and I want us to make this work even after I leave. I want to come

back over and over again until I retire, and then grow old together," Maxwell said.

Brick groaned and backed away. He'd talk if Maxwell
wanted to. In fact, he was excited that Maxwell had brought
it up. He just wished he'd done so after they'd had sex instead
of before.

*He's probably right, though. We should sort it out first. That'd
be the responsible thing to do.*

"Where are you going?" Maxwell asked. "I thought you had
needs." He wiggled his hips, seducing Brick back into position.

"Sorry. I thought you wanted to talk."

"Let's multitask," Maxwell said, looking at Brick and wag-
gling his eyebrows.

Brick certainly wasn't going to argue with that suggestion.
Even with the jeans between them, it had felt so good to slide
his dick against Maxwell's ass. "Okay," he said, stepping forward to press against Maxwell again. "But this seems to put me
at a certain disadvantage."

"I'm okay with that. I'll keep it short. I want us to make this
long-distance thing work out."

Brick couldn't stop himself from asking, "You sure? No
more guys from emails? You'll be back for Christmas?"

"As long as my leave gets approved. Only the Army can
keep me away from you now. No more guys. No more girls.
Just you. I'll do whatever it takes to make you believe it."

Brick rubbed the patch of exposed skin on the small of Maxwell's back. He wanted to get him completely out of that shirt and see the rest of him. "I trust you. So how do we make it work?"

Maxwell started gently bouncing his hips up and down, rubbing his ass along the length of Brick's cock. Brick gasped at the sensation.

I need to get him out of those pants.

"I don't know," Maxwell said. "I thought we could figure that out as we go. I just wanted us to commit to doing it for now. We can spend long, excruciating hours, completely dressed, sitting side by side and not touching each other tonight while we discuss it." He stopped bouncing his hips again. "Or we can just agree that it's what we both want to sort out soon and get to the fucking." He started his hips again, pressing back more firmly into Brick's body.

"The second one. More fucking. I need to be inside you, Maxwell."

Maxwell undid the buttons on his jeans.

When Brick heard the zipper, he didn't hesitate. He grabbed a condom and lube from his pocket before pushing his own pants down. Maxwell waited patiently, his pants already pulled down, but Brick didn't make him wait very long.

He quickly rolled the condom onto his dick. Rubbing the lube firmly into Maxwell earned him a sexy moan.

He tried to moderate his pace and gently push himself into

Maxwell, but Maxwell wasn't interested in taking it slowly either. He pushed his hips back once more, and Brick was inside him. The tightness was overwhelming.

"Fuck me, Brick. I need to be fucked hard and fast."

Brick didn't need any further encouragement. Any last semblance of self-control or boundaries disappeared. Maxwell was his and it was time for Brick to take what he wanted and give Maxwell what he asked for.

He grabbed Maxwell's hips and fucked him hard. They both grunted and screamed and called out each other's names, not caring who might hear their wild lovemaking.

As Brick wished it could go on forever, the reality that Maxwell would only be there a couple more days sank in, making Brick fuck harder in frustration at the cruelty of love.

Brick reached around and grabbed Maxwell's dick, to make sure his needs were taken care of, too, loving the feel of his boyfriend in his hand, and trying to memorize as much of Maxwell's body as he could so he'd be able to recall it whenever he needed to until Maxwell returned.

They were quickly covered with sweat. It felt like hours had passed without the release Brick needed, but as strong as his own lust was, he held himself back, trying to last long enough that Maxwell could come first.

Just when Brick didn't think he'd be able to make it, Maxwell called out, "I'm coming, you magnificent bastard!"

Brick felt Maxwell's dick pulse in his hand as he shot his load onto the bed.

Keeping his grip tight and continuing to milk the last drops from Maxwell, Brick continued slamming into him. Maxwell's grunts and moans were music to his ears.

When Brick finally exploded, the orgasm was stronger than any he'd ever had before. But that didn't really surprise him.

Everything was better with Maxwell.

He couldn't wait to see how amazing things would get as the years passed and they grew even closer together. Based on the short amount of time they had known each other, the thought of that kind of commitment was jarring, but, nevertheless, it felt right.

Still, the moment felt like it needed a little bit of levity before he went too far with things.

"You needed it hard and fast, huh?" Brick asked, feeling cocky in his afterglow.

"Sure did. I needed to get this wrapped up so I could go get that pop and maybe some chips. Want anything?"

Brick pulled Maxwell back against his body when he tried to get away. After a gentle bite on Maxwell's ear, Brick said, "Just you."

Maxwell smiled and kissed Brick. "That's so sweet."

Brick finally risked releasing Maxwell.

I could use some sugar to fuel up for the next round.

Before Maxwell made it to the door, Brick called out, "Get me a candy bar. Something with chocolate and peanut butter."

Maxwell stuck out his tongue and hurried out of the room.

Falling back on the bed, Brick couldn't believe that despite all the horrible things that had happened with Billy, the fling with Maxwell had managed to turn into something magical. Maybe Billy had helped bring them together stronger than they would have done on their own.

He still needs to be locked up until he's a very old man.

He rolled onto his side, facing the door, to wait for Maxwell to return with his candy bar so they could start round two. The exhaustion finally caught up to him, though. He fell asleep before Maxwell even returned.

When Nicole pounded on their door the next morning, they awoke in each other's arms.

Together.

CHAPTER 33

Maxwell

MAXWELL SAT IN THE BACK of the transport vehicle. He and the other soldiers were returning back to the base. They'd just finished a long, grueling mission through a little village where a known terrorist cell had taken residence. Fortunately, they'd managed to find them fairly easily. Instead of allowing himself to be taken prisoner, though, the leader had fought back, forcing the troops to kill him and his followers.

The chatter in the vehicle was loud and boisterous, as it always was after a successful mission. None of the troops had taken a single injury other than Keith, who'd rolled his ankle. Maxwell himself had taken out two of the guards before they'd even known the soldiers had entered the compound, which had gone a long way in making sure their mission had gone off so cleanly.

"...And then Maxwell here," Keith, sitting to Maxwell's right, said to the audience while patting Maxwell on the helmet. "This bastard shoots two guards with one bullet. Kills them dead with one fucking bullet."

Maxwell didn't bother to correct the exaggeration. He'd actually fired four shots. No one wanted to know the truth, though. The soldiers needed to believe they were at least a little invincible.

Maxwell shared their pride at completing the mission, but unlike the rest of the troops, he rode mostly in silence. He was happy they'd gotten their guy, and normally would have been as loud as anyone else, but on the trip back to the base all he could think about was how happy he was that none of his friends had been hurt.

After his visit over the summer with Brick, coming back safely from each mission was taking a much higher priority in Maxwell's mind. Now that he'd had a taste of happiness and real love, he was terrified of throwing it away by getting himself killed.

Even worse, if Maxwell was the one that died, Brick would

be the one that would have to suffer through losing the man he loved. So staying alive was really as much about protecting Brick as anything else.

I can't believe he loves me. What did I do to deserve him?

He was always able to push all his worries aside during the actual fighting, but the rides back afterward were getting rougher each time out. He still had a few months left on this enlistment and then another eight to twelve years before he'd really start thinking about retiring.

Each time he let himself think about reenlisting, he hated how much the Army was keeping him away from Brick and would continue to do so for years to come. Even if he wasn't deployed overseas, the odds were he wouldn't ever be stationed in the Midwest, and they'd still be forced into having a long-distance relationship for many more years.

With a sigh he forced himself to smile while the guys continued to boast about his magic shot and all their own exaggerated heroics all the way back to base.

When they arrived, Maxwell turned down the invitations to join the rest of the guys at the bar to celebrate. He'd drunk a little too much when he first returned to action after his visit with Brick, trying to hide the dark thoughts that came from being separated from someone who brought him such happiness.

Once he noticed what he was doing, he made sure to avoid

drinking unless he was happy, which meant he didn't drink very much anymore.

How can I be happy away from Brick?

Waving everyone goodbye and promising to go out with them next time, he stopped to check his mail on the way back to his bunk and was rewarded by a package from Brick. He nearly screamed with joy when he tore it open and saw the calendar inside.

His calendar. The Firefighters on the Fox.

He smiled at all the happy memories of taking pictures of the firefighters who had accepted him as their friend as he flipped through the pages. When it came to September, he started to cry, wishing once again that he could be home instead.

There was a newspaper clipping in the envelope, too. It showed a picture of Billy and mentioned that the trial had begun.

Brick wrote about how much stronger Nicole seemed these days. She'd testified against Billy and, according to Brick, had looked the bastard right in the eyes during most of her time being questioned.

She'd also asked if Brick had any friends that might be interested in going out dancing somewhere she could wear her red dress. Most surprisingly, she'd even started taking night classes to train to become a nurse.

Maxwell was happy to hear about things getting better for Nicole, but he wished Brick had written more about himself. They'd have to Skype again soon. Brick never had trouble talking about himself that way.

Maxwell set the picture underneath his pillow for the night. He'd hang it somewhere in the morning, but for the night, he wanted to sleep as close to Brick as he could.

EPILOGUE

Brick

Brick waited impatiently, idling in the pick-up lane at the airport, and hoping that no one would tell him he'd been sitting there too long. He didn't want to have to do the loop around the airport and try to find a spot again.

Maxwell was returning to spend his Christmas with Brick, and Brick didn't want to waste any of their limited amount of time trying to find each other in the chaos. Brick had big plans for their days together, and he wanted to make sure they made the most of it...by never leaving his house. He had menus from all the restaurants in town that delivered, and the refrigerator was full of various drinks to help them stay hydrated.

The car behind Brick honked. While he was checking his mirrors, the side door opened, startling him. "Jesus Christ."

"Glad to see you, too," Maxwell said with a huge grin across his face. "I had a little trouble finding my bag. I was just about to consider it lost and sort it all out later when it finally came down the conveyor belt. I need a soda, though. So let's stop at the first gas station or drive-through we find."

Brick wanted to do exactly two things.

Get home.

Make love.

Stopping anywhere along the way seemed like a needless waste of time. But rather than arguing about it, which would be an even stupider way to start their short time together, he leaned over for a kiss before pulling into traffic.

After stopping to get his drink, Maxwell made Brick stop at two other stores. He wanted a new bag to carry his camera from the first place, and a candy bar that he was suddenly craving from the second.

While nibbling on the candy bar, he said "Oh my God. This is so good. We don't get nearly enough chocolate in Afghanistan. Ooh. Can we stop at the mall on the way home? I want to look for some new shoes."

Brick's frustration finally started to bubble over. He slapped the steering wheel once before stopping himself and gripping it tightly enough to turn his knuckles white. "We could," he said through gritted teeth. "But do you really need shoes since you're only going to be here for a couple of days? Don't you think we should spend our time doing more interesting things? Things that don't require any shoes at all."

Maxwell looked down at his feet. "These are just so uncomfortable. If we go anywhere at all, I'm just going to be crabby thinking about how much my feet hurt. Just stop at the mall. It won't take more than an hour."

Suppressing a growl, Brick prepared to beg Maxwell to not go shopping.

Before he could, though, Maxwell started laughing, "I'm sorry. I'm just messing with you. I was just...well, here." Maxwell pulled a large, yellow envelope from his backpack and handed it to Brick.

"What is this?" Brick asked, giving it a glance before turning his attention back to the traffic.

"Oh, it's just my discharge papers. I decided I didn't want to spend any more time in the Army, so I didn't reenlist. So I'll be back forever now. I hope you won't get bored of me. But as long as you don't, we have all the time in the world."

"Like hell we do!" Brick shouted. "I need you home and in my bed more than ever now!"

Maxwell laughed. "I love your enthusiasm, Brick Swan."

Brick said, "I love that you found a way for us to be able to be together for real now."

"I love that you've clearly been lifting weights even more than usual since I've been gone," Maxwell said, squeezing the arm closest to him.

"I love that you've let your hair grow out enough for me to have something to grab ahold of when we're fucking."

Both men laughed and turned to each other at the same time, and said, "I love you."

Maxwell pointed at the front window. "Watch out!"

Brick slammed on his brakes in time to avoid hitting the car that had stopped at the red light in front of them. Brick focused more attentively on the road during the rest of the drive while they continued to name things they loved about each other.

As they pulled up to the house, Maxwell said, "Wow. The place looks brand new. I like the porch."

"I worked the crews like crazy to make sure it was ready for when you got back. I'm glad I pushed so hard. Now we have a good foundation to start the rest of lives with each other. I still can't believe you left the Army. "

"I had to. I couldn't survive spending any more time away from you."

The two entered the new house, holding hands, together.

The End

Get your free bonus scene from *Choice on Fire*

Not quite ready to leave Brick and Maxwell behind?

Sign up to the free Zach Jenkins' Fan Club to receive an exclusive bonus scene from *Choice on Fire* that's only available to registered fans.

All members will also receive free bonus scenes from future books as they become available.

Coming soon, members will receive an **exclusive Fan Club only standalone novella**! Join today to get notified as soon as it is available.

http://eepurl.com/b3CBzD

Also by Zach Jenkins

About the Author

Zach Jenkins was born in the Midwest and stayed in the Midwest until the military sent him bouncing from coast to coast and even overseas for four years. Having experienced some amazing places in this small world, he eventually settled back in the Midwest close to family and friends.

He spends most of his free time catching up with TV shows on Netflix and chasing his barking dogs away from the windows so the mailman will continue to deliver the frequent packages that Amazon keeps sending him.

Manufactured by Amazon.ca
Bolton, ON

26552873R00166